Promises and Lies

ROWENA SUDBURY

Dreamspinner Press

Published by
Dreamspinner Press
4760 Preston Road
Suite 244-149
Frisco, TX 75034
http://www.dreamspinnerpress.com/

Promises and Lies

Cover Art by Justin James   dare.empire@gmail.com
Cover Design by Mara McKennen

ISBN: 978-1-61581-641-5

Printed in the United States of America
First Edition
November, 2010

eBook edition available
eBook ISBN: 978-1-61581-642-2

For Mom, Dad, Dave, and Peter.
Your never-ending support means the world to me.

For Danyel and Sam.
Your quick minds keep me on my toes.

And for Jai.
Without you this story would never have been possible.

Chapter 1

The Park

SUN dappled through the trees, lending late spring warmth to Lullwater Park. Midday found mostly men on business lunches, new moms with strollers, and birds looking for handouts. Within a month the park would be given over to children let out from school's prison for the summer, but until then it was still a place for adults.

Sean Murphy liked the park. His demanding job kept him tied to a desk for long hours, and there was something about sitting outside in the sun that cleared his mind and helped him concentrate. It was his aim to meet his old friend Gabriel Romano for lunch here every other week, and when they were lucky, they met every week. The two had met while attending Emory University after they had drawn one another's names in the dormitory lottery and had become fast friends, sticking by each other through four years of ups and downs. Sean hadn't had a career path laid out, and it had been his goal to party as much as he could before earning his degree, while Gabriel's lifelong ambition had always been medicine.

After graduation, Sean had parlayed his military history degree into a job consulting with the U.S. government. Gabriel suffered an ugly breakup when he opted to return to his native Rhode Island to complete medical school, leaving his boyfriend Mark in the dust of a hot Atlanta summer.

Now, ten years later, the two were comfortably settled. Sean's keen knowledge of military strategy had set him on a career course that guaranteed success. Gabriel had returned from Rhode Island when his studies were complete and had set up his own practice. Their friendship remained intact.

The park was peaceful as Sean and Gabriel sat side by side on a bench, Gabriel's half in the shade but Sean's half fully in the sun. Gabriel picked chicken salad out of a plastic container, while Sean wolfed down the rest of a hamburger and flicked fries at the pigeons, smirking as they ran from the missiles and then cautiously came back to pick them up.

"So," Sean drawled when the fries were gone, "when were you planning to tell me you hooked up with Mark again?" He tipped his head back toward the sun, eyes closed behind his dark glasses.

"Didn't know I had to keep you posted with my life," Gabriel said as he snapped the lid back on the container and picked up his bottle of green tea.

"You back in the sack?"

"For fuck's sake, Sean," Gabriel sputtered, "that's a personal question. I contacted Mark, we revived the plans we'd long held, and we drew up a partnership. Peachtree Clinic was always meant to be a two-man show, and I know that I took on the practice with the hope that Mark would be my partner. Hell, it's the reason I moved back here."

Sean pushed himself up, straightened his necktie, and turned to face Gabriel. "Well, okay then, let me ask you this way. I know ten years is a long time, but I know what hell you two went through when you dumped him for greener pastures. You said he's your partner, so I'm just asking, does the partnership extend beyond the clinic?"

Gabriel screwed the cap back on the bottle of tea and tucked it inside his lunch sack. "Since you have to know, Mr. Busybody," he said with a hint of irritation, "Mark is my partner in the clinic only." He sighed, his face clouding as he remembered the details of the breakup. Although Gabriel had promised to wait a year after graduation so that the two of them could start med school together, he had broken the promise and gone ahead on his own. When he closed his eyes he could still remember the silvery tracks of Mark's tears the night he had broken the news to him. Gabriel cleared his throat before continuing, "Mark and I were able to sort out our differences, and if you must know, he's seeing some guy named Todd now."

"You okay with that?" Sean tipped his glasses down and fixed Gabriel with a steely look.

Sighing in frustration, Gabriel said, "I suffer these weekly lunches because you're too much of a bastard for me to cut you out of my life completely. Yes, Dr. Phil, I'm okay with it. He's moved on and doesn't carry a grudge, and you know I always let bygones be bygones."

Sean sat up and pulled the glasses off completely, a frown affixed to his brow.

"What?" Gabriel said. "You don't believe me?"

"No, it's not that...." Sean's voice trailed off.

Realizing that Sean wasn't giving him his full attention anymore, Gabriel turned and followed Sean's gaze. Two men had entered the park not far from where they sat. The younger of the pair wore tattered jeans and an old stretched T-shirt advertising a local band. His dark hair was streaked with blond and fell well past his shoulders. He held the leash of a frisky puppy. The older man by his side walked with hands shoved into his pockets. Oil-stained jeans and tattoos up and down the arms, visible outside a sleeveless jean jacket, gave the impression he was a biker. As they got closer, Sean and Gabriel were able to overhear their conversation.

"Not so tight, Jeff, let him run a little," said the older man in a gruff voice.

"I don't want him to get away, though, Jesse," said Jeff.

"He ain't going to get away," Jesse said. "Just wrap your hand around the leash."

"I know what I'm doing," Jeff muttered. "You know I'm not a kid anymore."

"I never said you were," Jesse said. "If that dog gets away, you won't never catch him."

Once they had walked past, Gabriel turned to resume his conversation with Sean but found that he was watching the two men and the dog with rapt attention. With a bemused look, Gabriel turned to watch them again, trying to see what had captured Sean's interest.

"Jesse," Jeff said as they paused beside the next bench, "can I please just walk with him by myself a little?"

Jesse sighed and eased down on the bench. "Just be careful, Jeff. You know this park is filled with assholes."

Jeff flinched, and he hunched in on himself. "I'll be careful. Besides, you're here watching me." He walked away toward the towering oak tree in the center of the park, and when he was halfway there, the dog slipped out of his leash and frolicked after one of the pigeons. In a split second, Sean was off the bench before Jesse could react. Gabriel sat dumbfounded as he watched Sean sprint after the dog, catch him, and, heedless of his business suit, carry him back to where Jeff had sunk to his knees in terror.

Gabriel stood when Jesse stood and went to lay a hand on his shoulder before he could start toward Jeff.

Flinching at the sudden contact, Jesse turned. "Get lost," he growled.

Gabriel cleared his throat. "No need to worry," he said. "Sean's impetuous, but he doesn't mean your friend any harm." He smiled and extended his hand. "Gabriel Romano, Peachtree Clinic."

"Listen, Peachtree Clinic," Jesse said, his hands clenching into fists, "I don't know you or that asshole from a hole in the ground."

A muscle tensed in Gabriel's jaw. "Sean Murphy's the top consultant with Koehler Industries, and he's got high-level security clearance. He's not your everyday run-of-the-mill stranger; it's just in his nature to help out when he can."

Although he made a move to follow after Jeff and Sean, Jesse muttered under his breath, "I got my eye on him."

"Fair enough," Gabriel responded. He waited until Jesse moved back to sit on the bench before he turned and sat on his own bench. As he watched, he wondered what Sean had gotten himself into this time.

After catching the puppy, Sean carried him over to where Jeff knelt on the ground.

"Easy, boy," Sean crooned as he gentled the puppy.

"His name's Dakotah," Jeff said breathlessly.

"That's a nice name," Sean said, and he slipped the collar over the dog's head and tightened it up a notch. "There you go, Kotah, good as new."

"That's what I call him too!" Jeff said.

"What?" Sean said as he turned toward Jeff, "Kotah?"

"Yeah, 'cause it's easier to say sometimes," Jeff said, soft color covering his cheeks, and he dipped his head and mumbled, "Thanks, mister, for catching him and all."

"My name's Sean, and it was no trouble."

"You're going to get your pants all dirty," Jeff said, his head still bent, his hands gripping the leash. "I got him now."

"Eh," Sean said, "pants can be cleaned." He tipped his head to the side. "I know the dog's name, but not yours."

"It's Jeff." He cast a look over his shoulder. "Look, I better get back over to Jesse."

"Okay, I'll walk you over." Sean stood and dusted off his knees.

As Jeff stood, something dropped out of his pocket. Sean bent down, picked it up, and saw it was a toy plastic soldier. He grinned and said, "This yours?"

His face scarlet now, Jeff reached over and snatched the soldier from Sean's hand. "No, I mean"—he looked up, his face filled with uncertainty—"I found it on the ground, and I was going to throw it away."

"That's a ground combat soldier," Sean said. "You can tell because of the pack he's got on his back. That's where he keeps his supplies, rations, maybe a radio. I wouldn't throw it away if I were you."

"How do you know?" Jeff asked as he ran his thumb over the soldier.

"It's my job," Sean said, "designing gear for the army, helping with strategies." He smiled. "And it's my hobby, collecting model soldiers. I have a whole army of them back at my house."

Dakotah pranced ahead of them as they walked back toward where Gabriel and Jesse sat on the benches. Jeff still held the toy soldier in his hand.

"Put your toys away, Jeff," Jesse said as he reached for the end of the leash. "Time to go home."

"It's not a toy," Sean said firmly. "It's a model."

"Thanks… Sean." Jeff looked up shyly.

"Maybe I'll see you here again sometime. You bring more of those models, and I'll tell you all about them," Sean said with a smile that was clearly only for Jeff.

"Thanks for your help, Murphy," Jesse said shortly, "but you won't be seeing him here again."

"I think that's up to him," Sean said, and he turned and winked at Jeff. He grinned as Jeff attempted to return the wink but closed both eyes.

Jesse grabbed the leash from Jeff's hand, nodded curtly at Sean and Gabriel, and as he turned away, they heard him say, "Come on, Jeff, let's get this dog home and have us some lunch. And put that toy away before I take it away."

After they walked away, Gabriel began to pick up the remains of his and Sean's lunch. "What was that all about?"

"Something ain't right there," Sean said as he wadded up his bags.

"Maybe so," Gabriel said, "but it's none of your business."

"Now see," Sean said as he put his glasses back on and clapped an arm around Gabriel's shoulder, "if everyone in the world stayed out of everyone's business, all kinds of shit would go down. That kid needs a savior."

"Here we go again," Gabriel said as he shrugged out of Sean's arm. "Hate to burst your bubble, Sean, but you can't be everyone's savior, and chances are you won't ever see him again."

"Maybe," Sean said with a laugh, "maybe not. You know the old saying—'where there's a will, there's a way.' Besides," he said with a shrug, "you know me, just trying to make the world a better place, one asshole at a time."

Gabriel smirked. "Since when?"

"Since I realized the world is filled with them."

Chapter 2

Reluctant

JESSE shifted uncomfortably on the hard chair, watching as the court-appointed doctor leafed through Jeff's thick file. In his eyes, this was one final step before their lives returned to some semblance of normalcy.

At last, the papers neatly stacked, the doctor looked up. "What is your relation to Mr. Hayes?"

With an exaggerated sigh of irritation, Jesse said, "It's all in the affidavit I gave when he was in the hospital. I am his guardian."

Frowning, the doctor said, "But Mr. Hayes is long past the age of majority."

"You saw him," Jesse said with a snort. "Does he look like he can live on his own?"

"Mental illness is a tricky thing," the doctor said, "and as such, I agree he is better off with a caregiver."

"He ain't mentally ill," Jesse said irritably. "He's got quirks is all." He shifted again and eyed the clock on the wall behind the doctor's desk.

"He isn't very talkative," the doctor said, "but what I've gleaned from the few things he has told me, and what you have told me, he's suffering from post-traumatic stress coupled with the final throes of drug addiction. My advice is for him to begin a course of treatment."

"No," Jesse said. "I'll take care of him myself."

"I'd advise against it. He was evasive when I asked him about the needle tracks on his arms, but blood tests show traces of heroin in his system. While he was hospitalized, the worst of the withdrawal occurred; however, he should be monitored. It isn't just the physical aspects he needs to get past but the emotional ones as well."

Jesse sat forward. "The last thing Jeff needs is you poking and prodding at him. He'll snap out of it eventually, and then I'll let him come and work with me in my shop. I'll make sure he don't fall in with the wrong crowd again."

"Jeff needs to establish his own boundaries. He's not a child. If you try to control him, he'll 'fall in with the wrong crowd,' as you put it, faster than you can blink an eye. I'd like to see him once a week until his mental condition stabilizes."

"He ain't got a mental condition," Jesse said as he stood. "And like you said, he's not a child. Where I come from, we deal with problems ourselves. All he has to do is man up, and working with me and the boys in the shop, that'll set him straight. Guaranteed he don't want no shrink."

"Mr. Conway," the doctor said as he stood and walked around the edge of his desk, "I strongly recommend that you bring him in for psychiatric evaluation."

"Listen," Jesse said angrily, "unless the law states specifically that I have to bring him to a shrink, I'm not going to. Way I understood it, that choice was up to Jeff and me. I know Jeff don't want it, and I don't either. I don't plan on being his guardian forever, just until he gets back on his feet."

Sighing in resignation, the doctor turned to close Jeff's file. "I will make a note that treatment was refused."

"Damn straight," Jesse said. "We done here?"

"Yes," the doctor said, "you are free to go."

Jesse collected Jeff from the waiting room, and together they walked out to Jesse's beat-up pickup truck.

"The doc thinks you got a mental condition," Jesse said as he pulled out of the lot and headed toward the home he and Jeff shared. "He wants you to go see him once a week so you can get over it."

"I ain't crazy," Jeff mumbled.

"I know that," Jesse said. "I told the quack that. The cuts are healed, and all you need now is to get your strength back. Then you can come work with me in the shop."

Jeff winced at the casual mention of the cuts, and he said softly, "I don't want to build choppers, Jesse."

"Yeah, well, what do you want to do, then? Lay in your room all day and draw pictures? That's a waste of time, Jeff, and you know it. Real men build things with their hands, get their hands dirty. If you plan on living with me and letting me provide for you, then you'll work in the shop with me," Jesse said as he pulled up into the driveway of their home.

"Luke don't get his hands dirty," Jeff said as they walked up the front walkway.

"Your brother's a pansy," Jesse said. "Reading books all day is as bad as drawing pictures."

"But Luke teaches," Jeff said.

Jesse snorted. "Like I said, real men work with their hands. Besides, Luke don't have no time for us now. Go and wash up. I'll get dinner ready."

"I can fix the dinner," Jeff said, brightening.

"Nah, you go and feed that mutt, wash your hands, lay down for a spell, and I'll let you know when the grub's fixed."

With a sigh, Jeff wandered out into the yard. Dakotah leaped up and licked his cheek and frisked around him as he poured food into his bowl.

"I wish you could come in the house, Kotah," Jeff said, "but Jesse won't let me bring you in." He bent down and put his arms around the dog's neck. "Someday we're going to have our own house, you 'n' me. And then you can sleep on the bed and all kinds of things. Okay?"

Dakotah wriggled out of Jeff's arms and scampered over to start eating. Jeff smiled ruefully and went back into the house.

Jeff's room was up front. It had been his room since he had come to live with Jesse many years earlier. The walls were lined with his drawings, intricate, detailed pictures of knights and dragons. He had tacked a colorful parachute up on the ceiling, and it made the room feel like a tent. He reached into his pocket and took the toy soldier out, carefully set it on the shelf with the others.

The bad memories that welled up every time he twisted the wrong way and fiery pain tore across his hip were quelled somewhat as he thought about his encounter with the man in the park the day before.

"His name was Sean," he whispered as he flopped back on the bed. "And he said they're not toys, they're models."

Jeff lay still and watched the parachute lift and fall in the breeze coming through the open window. Instead of falling into the numbness of forgetting, he allowed himself to think about the handsome man in the park. Somehow he'd get back there, maybe when Jesse was at work.

Chapter 3

Determined

SEAN pecked out a response on his BlackBerry as he sat in the sun on the park bench with his sleeves rolled up, tie loosened, and his jacket slung carelessly over the back of the bench.

"It keeps my head clear," he typed in an e-mail response. "Get claustrophobic cooped up in the office all day."

He smirked as he sent the e-mail. That wasn't the complete truth, but it was close enough. Truth was he had been back at Lullwater every day hoping for a glimpse of the boy and his dog. Atlanta was a big place, and he knew the chances were slim, but something drew him to those melancholy green eyes, the memory of long hair streaked with blond and black, the graceful curve of ass in jeans. He chided himself as he slipped the phone back into his pocket. Chances were the kid had a girlfriend.

It had been years since Sean had been exclusive with anyone. When he and Gabriel were in college, he'd had one steady partner. Andy had matched Sean in stamina and demeanor. There had been many a night where Andy wheedled Sean into writing a paper for him and then spent the night "paying" for it. Sean always knew in the back of his head that Andy wanted commitment, but he'd never given it. In Sean's opinion, the world was a smorgasbord, and the more he tasted, the more he wanted.

As time went on, he had chided himself that he wasn't getting any younger. Currently he wasn't seeing anyone, and even the allure of the clubs had lost its luster. Although he had tried to maintain a friendship with Andy, it had never worked. It still amazed him that Gabriel and Mark could coexist at the same clinic. Whenever he badgered Gabriel about it, though, he was told tightly it was an issue of maturity.

Out of the corner of his eye, Sean caught a movement, and he turned to watch as Jeff entered the park with Dakotah in tow. He was by himself this time, and he held the leash with both hands. Sean leaned forward, his forearms resting on his knees as he watched Jeff give all his attention to the dog, and as they got closer, he could hear Jeff's singsong voice as he talked.

"It's okay, Kotah," he said softly, "there ain't no pigeons here today, see?"

Sean smiled, sitting quietly as they approached, and then he said, "Well if it isn't my favorite dog." He dug in his pocket and withdrew a dog biscuit. "Here Kotah, brought it just for you."

Jeff gasped and looked up, startled. Dakotah lunged forward, his tail beating against Jeff's leg. Jeff walked closer and let Dakotah take the treat. "How did you know I'd be here today?"

"I didn't," Sean said. "That's why I've been coming here every day since I saw you last week."

"Really?" Jeff asked, his cheeks going pink.

Sean's phone buzzed, and he reached into his pocket to silence the ringer. "Really. You by yourself?"

"Yeah." Jeff dipped his head and shifted his weight from one foot to the other. "Jesse got tied up at work."

Sean slid down the bench and patted the space next to him. "He your dad?"

Jeff looked over his shoulder and then turned back and eased down on the bench. "He's my guardian."

Dakotah rolled under the bench and ate the biscuit.

"Can I ask you a question, Jeff?" Sean asked. "You don't have to answer, but I'm just curious. How old are you?"

"Twenty-three," Jeff whispered.

"Then what do you need with a guardian? I mean, seems like you could look after yourself."

Jeff was quiet for a moment, and then he said, "I went to live with him when my folks were killed in a car wreck, and I've just lived with him ever since. I don't got a job or nothing, and Luke has his own life, so I just stay with Jesse."

"Luke?" Sean transferred his phone from his pocket to his briefcase. Work would wait for the rest of the day.

"My brother," Jeff said.

"Well, look, I'm not trying to pry into your life or anything," Sean said, "it's just that, you know, I like you."

Jeff closed his eyes, and a pained look crossed his features. "I better go," he said.

"Why? You just got here."

"Because I know what you mean, and I know what you want," Jeff said as he opened his eyes.

Sean frowned. "I don't follow you. What do I want?"

"Last time a man said 'I like you' when he didn't know me, he wanted to hurt me," Jeff said as he stood up.

"Hold on a minute," Sean said as he stood. "I said I like you because I liked talking to you last time about the soldiers. Most people don't give a crap about military strategy, but it's my life. Now I reckon I can guess what you're driving at, but I'll tell you straight up that's not what I'm after." He cocked his head to the side. "I was hoping you brought another one of those soldiers."

"No, I didn't," Jeff said, and he wrapped the end of the leash around his hand.

"Well, I did," Sean said. He reached into his briefcase again and pulled out a model of a World War II soldier. "I made this one, and it turned out it was a duplicate for one I already had, so I figured you might like it."

Jeff stared at the soldier and then looked back up at Sean. "You brought that for—"

"I brought it for you," Sean said, and he smiled.

"He's...." Jeff hesitated, and then he smiled. "He's nicer than the ones I have." Absently, he reached for the model and settled back on the bench.

"He's just different, is all," Sean said. "See, he's got netting on his helmet and a pack, like your soldier, but he's also got an ammo belt and a rifle."

"Yeah, but," Jeff ran his thumb over the soldier, "he's not plastic."

Sean shrugged. "Plastic, metal, it don't matter; they're still soldiers."

"How do you know all this stuff about soldiers?" Jeff asked.

"I studied military history in school. It's something I've always been interested in, soldiers and fighting." Sean leaned back against the bench.

"Me too," Jeff said, "only I like medieval knights and King Arthur, stuff like that."

"They make models like that," Sean said. "I could show you how, help you make one."

"I don't know," Jeff said. "I still, I mean," he paused and looked at Sean. "Why?"

Sean cocked his head to the side. "No strings attached, Jeff," he said softly. "I heard what you said before, and I'm guessing you've been taken advantage of. If I wanted something from you, I'd just ask you."

Jeff tightened his hand on Dakotah's leash. "I better go, for real this time."

"Okay," Sean said. He reached in his pocket again and this time took out a business card. "Look, here's my number, that's my cell. Just call me if you want to talk, or we can meet up here again some time."

Jeff took the card as Dakotah crawled out from under the bench. He put the card carefully away in his pocket and continued to hold the soldier in his hand. "I can come when Jesse gets busy at work." He shifted his weight from one foot to the other and said, "He didn't tell me not to come, but I don't think he likes me going out by myself."

"Like I told you, kiddo," Sean said, "twenty-three's plenty old enough to make your own decisions." He winked.

"I know," Jeff murmured.

"Then it's a promise?" Sean said.

"Yeah, a promise." Jeff smiled, and then he turned and walked back the way he'd come, Dakotah walking docilely at his side.

Chapter 4

Breaking the Ice

"I DON'T get it, Sean," Gabriel said as they shared lunch again a few weeks later. "Since when do you feel you need to save the world?"

Sean shrugged and leaned back on the bench. "I don't, Gabe."

"Then why this drive to see this kid here every week? How many times has it been since that first time?"

"He's not a kid, and this man he lives with is an asshole. Don't set right with me." Sean pulled his phone out of his pocket, checked the screen, then set it aside again. "I've met him here a few times since then."

"You looking to score with him or something?" Gabriel asked.

"That's an awfully crude way to put it," Sean growled. "Maybe it ain't any of your fucking business."

"Oh, so it's okay for you to grill me about my private life with Mark, but it's not okay for me to ask you about your designs on a stranger." Gabriel tipped his head to the side. "Is this kid even gay?"

Rather than fly off the handle, Sean said, "I haven't really come right out and asked him, but from what I gather from bits and pieces, he's said he is. Sounds like he was a hustler, or someone's pet, something like that. He said he dropped out of high school and got involved in something he's not too comfortable talking about; I don't push him."

Gabriel closed his eyes and ran a hand over his brow. "What happened to the real Sean Murphy, huh?" he asked. "That guy who used to have a series of one-night stands with men he picked up at clubs? You don't sound like you."

"I changed," Sean said matter-of-factly. "Maybe I want to see how the other half lives."

"The other half doesn't pick up boys in the park and talk about soldiers with them," Gabriel said sternly.

"Look," Sean said, a frown marring his brow, "I'll take your concern the way you intend it, but this is the last time I'm going to say it. Jeff isn't a boy, and I am taking this for what it's worth. Hell, maybe next week he'll quit coming, and this will all be a moot point." He put on his sunglasses, stood, and shouldered into his jacket. "I quit harassing you about Mark; it's the least you could do to lay off about Jeff."

"I just hope you know what you're doing," Gabriel said as he stood. He pulled Sean into a bear hug.

"I love you, too, man," Sean said as he broke the hug.

SEAN settled into a routine with Jeff. They met in the park once a week, and Sean made sure it was not on the same day he met with Gabriel. Jeff left each time promptly at three and always refused to let Sean drive him home. Sean knew that Jeff left in time to be home before Jesse, but he let it go. He just continued to remind Jeff that he could make his own decisions.

One afternoon Sean arrived at the park to find that Jeff was not waiting at the bench like he usually was. He frowned as he scanned the immediate area. The frown cleared when he found Jeff sitting underneath the oak tree with Dakotah stretched out beside him. He walked over and crouched down beside him, seeing that he was working on a drawing.

"What are you doing?" he said, but before he could take in the details of the drawing, Jeff clutched it up against his chest.

"I'm not wasting time," Jeff said, "honest!"

"I didn't say you were wasting time, Jeff," Sean said, and he eased down to sit beside him. "I just wanted to see the picture is all."

Jeff continued to clutch the drawing protectively against his chest; Dakotah stood and pushed his nose against Sean's hand, his tail wagging. Sean grinned, pulled a dog treat from his pocket, and murmured, "You're incorrigible, Kotah. What happens when I don't bring you a treat one day, hmm?" He looked back over at Jeff. "So?"

Reluctantly, Jeff lowered the picture, still holding it so that Sean couldn't see it clearly. "I was goin' from memory," he murmured.

Sean scooted around and looked at the sketchpad. It was a detailed, wild drawing of a knight engaged in battle; his sword arced high in the air, his opponent cowering before him. Around the outside edges were scenes of the larger battle that raged around the rampant knight. Looking closer, Sean noticed the cowering opponent strongly resembled Jesse. He shifted his gaze back to the main knight and drew in his breath. He reached over and ran his thumb lightly over the drawing.

"He looks like me," he said softly.

"It is you, Sean," Jeff said. "Or it's supposed to be you, anyway." He looked down at his hands clasped together in his lap and whispered, "My shining knight in armor."

"Jeff, this is really good," Sean said reverently. "Have you taken art classes?"

"Nah," Jeff said. "I just draw what's in my head."

Sean handed the pad back to Jeff, not wanting to pry into his thoughts by leafing through the rest of the pages. He smiled. "You said you liked these medieval knights, I guess you really do. I'm heading over to the model shop after this. Want to come with and get you a model of a knight?"

Jeff closed up the pad and fidgeted with the cover. "I don't know, Sean. I shouldn't—"

"Well," Sean said as he stood, "I'm going to go now, and you can come with me if you want."

After a moment's hesitation, Jeff stood. "It's only around two o'clock, right?"

Sean checked his watch. "Not even quite two yet," he said.

"Okay, then," Jeff said hesitantly, "but I gotta be home by three."

"I'll make sure you're home in time," Sean said.

They left Dakotah in the back of Sean's SUV with the windows cracked when they arrived at the store. "He's in the shade," Sean said, "and we won't be in there too long. I know right where the models are."

True to his word, they purchased the model and were back to the SUV in ten minutes. After some prodding, Jeff gave Sean his address, and Sean started the drive home. Jeff held the model in his lap and looked at it solemnly.

"How 'bout next week you come to my house," Sean said casually as he threaded his way through traffic. "I'll help you put it together."

Jeff chewed his lip and didn't answer.

Sean slowed down and pulled over to the side of the street. "Look, your house is right around the corner." He twisted his GPS unit to show Jeff where the star marked the final destination. "See that house right there?" He pointed across the street. "That's my place. Who knew we lived so close together? You can walk over here easily and still be home before Jesse gets home."

"Well," Jeff said slowly, and then he paused for so long Sean thought he meant to decline the invitation. "I guess I can come over."

"Good." Sean grinned. He pulled back out in traffic and completed the short drive to Jeff's house. "I'll see you next week, then."

"See you," Jeff said, and he managed a smile.

THE following week, Sean worked from home on the day they had arranged for Jeff to come over and build his model. He dressed casually, comfortably, in worn jeans that hugged every curve and an old T-shirt faded from many washings. His house was small, two bedrooms, one bathroom, and a detached garage at the end of a long driveway. The smaller of the two bedrooms was where he slept, and he used the other for a workshop. He set Jeff's model out on the table and pulled up two stools.

Jeff knocked on the door a little after noon with his sketchpad tucked under his arm and Dakotah on a leash. He chewed his lip when Sean opened the door. "I hope you don't mind I brought Kotah."

Sean grinned and said, "He's housebroken?" He stood back to let them inside.

"I don't know," Jeff said. "Jesse won't let me bring him inside the house."

"Tell you what, then. We'll keep him in the kitchen, and I'll leave the back door open so he can go out if he wants to."

"Okay," Jeff said with a smile.

After the dog was settled, Sean led Jeff into his workroom. Jeff sucked in his breath as he looked around the room. The centerpiece was a table covered with a mock battle scene. Everything was scaled down, but it all looked accurate. Along the wall was a desk with a large computer monitor and keyboard.

"It's my layout for this online game I participate in," Sean said with pride. "It's a role-playing game where everyone has a character, and we live the lives of these Civil War soldiers. A lot of the guys built their own models, so I did too. Right now we're re-enacting the Battle of Chancellorsville. It was a short one that only took four days."

Jeff bent down to study the model board. "Wow," he whispered. "And then what happens when that battle is done?"

"We decide on the next battle, take a few days to set up, then work through that one."

"Sounds like fun," Jeff said. He laid his sketchbook aside as he walked around the table and looked at the mock battlefield from all angles.

"It keeps me busy," Sean said. He sat on one of the stools by the side table, where Jeff's model was laid out.

When Jeff was done studying the large model, he came and perched on the stool by Sean's side.

"I'm glad you came today, Jeff," Sean said.

"Me too," Jeff said as he dipped his head.

"You hungry? We could eat before we start," Sean said.

"I ate before I came over," Jeff replied, "but you could eat if you're hungry."

"Nah, I'm fine," Sean said. He spun around on his stool and indicated the medieval knight model he had laid out. "You ready?"

Jeff turned and looked at the pieces of the model. "I didn't know it had so many parts," he said.

"It's not so many," Sean assured him. "Your first step is to catalogue all the parts. I already did that for you, so next you have to trim the edges down so they're smooth." He picked up a knife. "I'll show you."

Jeff moved back and whispered, "I can't use a knife."

Sean frowned. "Sure you can. See? It's not that hard." He skillfully trimmed the edges of the small piece, set it down, and picked up another.

"No," Jeff said, "I mean… the knife is too sharp."

Sean frowned and set the knife and the model piece down. "I don't get it," he said.

Jeff swallowed hard and closed his eyes. He clenched his hands together and said, "I hurt myself really bad with a knife."

"You want to tell me about it?" Sean asked.

Jeff gave one little shake of his head. "I… can't."

Sean took a deep breath. "Okay, then I'll prep the pieces, and you can tell me what you know about these battles the knights fought in."

Slowly, Jeff opened his eyes and watched as Sean worked on the model. He began to talk, telling Sean about the knights and battles. They fell into an easy camaraderie, and talk moved from knights and battles to movies and food until Jeff gasped.

"It's three thirty."

Sean set the last of the model pieces down and glanced up at the wall clock. "Shit, I lost track of time." He wiped his hand on a towel and said, "Let me drive you home."

Jeff slid down from the stool and went to the kitchen to get Dakotah. "Just walk over with me, Sean," he said. He took a deep breath. "I guess it's time Jesse knew."

"I like the sound of that," Sean said with a smile.

Jesse was waiting when they got there, arms crossed over his chest. Sean listened while Jeff explained where he'd been and that he would be spending more time with Sean while they built the model, impressed that Jeff seemed to have finally found a backbone.

Although Jesse kept the sneer firmly affixed on his face, he mumbled that it was okay as long as Jeff was home before dark, but he grabbed Sean's arm as he turned to leave and held him back.

"You try anything with him, Murphy, anything at all, and I'll hand you your ass before you even know it's even missing."

"Harsh words," Sean said with a smirk. "We're just building models, not nuclear bombs."

Jesse released his grip and snarled, "I didn't just fall off the turnip truck. All I'm saying is that it won't take much to figure out where you live." He eyed Sean and said in a soft voice, "Boy's been through a lot."

"He's not a boy. Whatever he's been through, I'm sure he'll tell me in time. Until then, don't get your shorts in a bunch, I don't mean him any harm." Sean kept his steely gaze fixed on Jesse for a moment, then turned and caught up with Jeff by the door. He took his hand to shake it. "See you tomorrow?"

Jeff smiled and nodded.

More bits and pieces of the puzzle fell into place the more Sean spent time with Jeff, and brief encounters with Jesse helped fill in the blanks. Jeff had "been through a lot," Jesse said. That fell in line with Sean's belief that Jeff had been taken advantage of by some man or men. Even though Jeff was old enough to live on his own, Jesse still seemed to have some kind of control over him. Because Jeff seemed so tentative about so many things, it made sense that he allowed it, but Sean still didn't like or understand it.

When he returned home, Sean went to straighten up in the workroom while he pondered over the encounter. Jeff's sketchbook was lying on the table where he'd left it. Sean picked it up and ran his thumb over the cover. He knew he should respect Jeff's privacy and set it aside until he could return it the next day, but once the room was set to rights, he picked it up and carried it out to the living room.

He settled in his favorite chair and turned on the light. After taking a deep breath, he opened the book and began to look at the magic Jeff had spilled out on the pages. Many of the figures had familiar faces; there was even one knight that bore a remarkable resemblance to Gabriel. Sean marveled at Jeff's talent for remembering faces.

At last he came to the picture he had seen Jeff drawing in the park, the fierce knight locked in battle with an evil knight. Along the sidelines of the battle stood a small figure that looked like Jeff, and Sean smiled as he realized the meaning of the picture, remembering that Jeff had called him a "shining knight in armor." He found it endearing the way Jeff sometimes twisted words around so that they weren't in the expected order.

He turned the page and gasped, his fingers gripping the book tighter. This picture showed the knight again, the one with his face. He was sprawled back under a tree, his head tipped back and an enraptured look on his face. The knight was naked this time, his engorged cock snug up against his belly. Crouched between his legs was the small figure from the sidelines of the battle, hands on the knight's knees, as he seemed to settle closer.

Although he knew he should close the book and put it aside, he couldn't help but turn the page. He groaned as he looked at the next picture, feeling himself harden within the confines of his jeans. In this picture, the small figure with Jeff's features held the tip of the knight's cock between his lips, and the knight had reached down to tangle his fingers in the small figure's hair. The eroticism of the image was palpable, and it was all Sean could do to tear his eyes from it and close the book.

Sean set the book aside and reached up to snap off the light. Had Jeff left the book as an invitation, or was Sean invading his inner thoughts by looking at it?

There was only one way to find out.

Chapter 5

Awakening

ALL through the night, Sean debated with himself. He could leave the book in the open and let Jeff discover he had forgotten it, or he could just hand the book to Jeff and be honest about the fact that he had looked at it. Something told him that he needed to tread carefully with Jeff. If he tried to push him or was dishonest, then in all likelihood Jeff would stop coming. That was clear after Jeff made the decision to tell Jesse that he was seeing Sean. It wasn't until after Sean stopped riding him about it that Jeff had made that decision.

When Jeff arrived the next day, Sean smiled and said, "I made us some lunch."

Jeff smiled tentatively as he followed Sean into the kitchen and found lunch set out on the table. "Thanks, Sean. You didn't have to."

"I know," Sean said as he pulled out Jeff's chair, "but I wanted to. I even got a bag of chow for Kotah."

Dakotah frisked down the back stairs and out into the yard to find the bowl of dog food, and Sean sat at the table with Jeff. "Turkey with Swiss cheese, and I didn't know if you liked potato chips or veggies, so I got both."

"Didn't know you cooked," Jeff said as he reached for a carrot.

"I don't," Sean said, "but anyone can make a sandwich."

Jeff gave him a wistful look and took a bite of carrot.

"Want a beer?" Sean asked. The kitchen was small; he pushed his chair back and opened the refrigerator.

"I don't drink," Jeff said.

Sean arched a brow and took out two bottles of water.

They ate in silence for a few minutes, and then Sean turned and took the sketchbook off the counter and laid it in front of Jeff. "You left this here yesterday," he said.

Jeff's eyes widened, and he looked from the book to Sean. "Did you... look at it?"

Sean dipped his head and murmured, "Yes, Jeff. I know it was an invasion of your privacy, but I looked at it." He raised his head and met Jeff's gaze. "Most of it, anyway."

"Oh," Jeff said. He pushed his plate away and pulled the book closer to him.

"I'm sorry, Jeff," Sean said. "It's just, you're a good artist. And even though I know you said you drew what was in your head, and I don't have any right to know what's in your head unless you tell me, I wanted to see that picture you drew of me again. I ain't gonna lie; I wanted to see if there were any more of them."

Soft color washed over Jeff's cheeks, but he remained silent.

"I only looked at two more pages after that," Sean said, "and they were beautiful."

Jeff looked down at the book, and when he spoke, Sean could hardly hear him. "Then you know what's in my head, Sean. You know what I want, even though I don't think I'm really ready for it. Not yet, anyway."

"Jeff, listen," Sean said, and he scooted his chair closer. "I'll be honest with you. Typically I'm not the kind of person to wait around for the right time. When I see something or someone I want, I just go for it. You know, shoot first and ask questions later. But that's not what I want with you. Those things that are in your head, they're in my head, too, but that don't mean I'm gonna make you suck me off right here, right now."

Although he wanted to touch Jeff, he kept his hands to himself and touched with his voice only. "If those things are in your head, well maybe one day they'll be a reality, but only when you want them to be. It's just, I want you to know that"—he paused and took a deep breath—"making them a reality is something I want too."

Jeff kept his head bent, his face turned away from Sean. "I never"—he paused—"I mean I ain't used to that, Sean. I'm used to guys just taking what they want from me."

"Then this is new ground for both of us," Sean said softly. "I'm used to just taking, too, but I don't want to this time."

Slowly Jeff turned toward Sean and raised his head to meet Sean's eyes. "I believe you, Sean."

Sean smiled and slid his hand along the table, close but not touching Jeff's hand quite yet. After a minute, Jeff reached up and touched his fingers to Sean's. For a moment they just looked into each other's eyes, and then Sean sat back as if he was afraid he couldn't hold his raging emotions in check.

"Ready to work on that model now?"

Jeff grinned. "Yeah. I am."

JEFF came to Sean's house every day after that, usually later in the afternoon after Sean's workday was over. The model was completed in a week, and Sean bought a few more. He cleared room on his main display table, and they started a medieval battle scene. Sean showed Jeff how his online role-playing game worked and let him watch a few of the battles. Some days they sat and talked, or Jeff drew in his sketchbook while Sean worked on contracts he had brought home from the office.

One afternoon they sat in the living room, Jeff with his sketchbook in his lap and Sean with his laptop. The sky was overcast, and it would rain before the day was over. Sean saved his work and looked over to where Jeff sat with his chin propped in his hand as he stared out the window.

"What are you thinking about, Jeff?" Sean asked.

Startled from his reverie, Jeff gasped and picked up his pencil. "Nothing."

"Looked like you were dreaming," Sean said quietly.

"Dreaming's a waste of time," Jeff muttered. He didn't start in on his drawing again.

"Everyone dreams, even me sometimes," Sean said, head cocked to the side as he once again tried to figure out what went on in Jeff's head. He closed the cover of the laptop and set it aside.

"For real?" Thunder rumbled off in the distance, and Jeff tensed. He closed his sketchbook and set it aside, hands clasped together in his lap.

"Yeah, for real," Sean said. "What's the matter?"

"I don't...." Jeff hesitated. "I don't like thunder."

Sean smiled and said, "We get a lot of it around here."

"I know," Jeff said. "But it always scares me, 'specially in the middle of the night."

The thunder was closer now, and lightning streaked across the sky. Jeff pulled his feet up on the couch and hugged his knees against his chest. Sean watched, and then he got up and went over to sit beside Jeff on the couch.

"Only one way to shut the thunder out," Sean said softly. He took a deep breath. "We can make some popcorn, and I'll read you a book."

A loud crack of thunder and a bright flash of lightning plunged the room into semi-darkness as the power went out. Jeff made a small whimper, and as if it were the most natural thing in the world, he pitched himself toward Sean. Sean raised his arm and let Jeff settle in close beside him. He bent down and pressed his lips against the top of Jeff's head. "Shh," he crooned, "it's okay."

"'M sorry Sean," Jeff whispered, "for being such a baby."

"Hush, Jeff," Sean said. "Will you let me get a candle and a book? It'll only take a minute."

"Okay," Jeff said. He eased back and watched as Sean sat forward and dug a candle out of the drawer on the end table. When it was lit, the soft orange glow filled up the darkness. He watched as Sean stood and crossed to a bookshelf, picked a book, and then came and sat back down.

"Where were we?" Sean asked, and he raised his arm.

Jeff snuggled back up against him. "Right here."

Sean opened the book. "The Jungle Book," he said, and then he began to read.

Rain had started, and it lashed the windows. Sean read, his rich voice covering the sound of the storm as he created the magic jungle. The thunder retreated, but the rain kept falling. At last Sean stopped and said softly, "It's late." He set the book aside, then put his arm more comfortably around Jeff. "Would you stay tonight? I don't think the thunder is gone, and I don't want you over at your house being afraid."

"Jesse...," Jeff said, and then he twisted to gaze up at Sean. He took a deep breath, and then he said, "Okay. Just let me call him, and tell him where I am."

Jeff made his call, and from the half of the conversation that Sean could hear, he knew that it took a little convincing on Jeff's part. Jeff stood his ground, and when he was done, they ate cheese and crackers by candlelight in the kitchen. Sean made a bed of old towels on the kitchen floor for Dakotah and then led Jeff to his bedroom. It was the first time Jeff had seen the inside of the room. The bed took up most of the floor space; the only other furniture was a dresser and a standing mirror.

"Just to sleep, Jeff," Sean murmured. He pulled back the covers on the bed and then stripped down to his briefs. Leaving Jeff to follow, he climbed into the bed and waited.

After a moment's hesitation, Jeff slipped his shoes and jeans off and then got into the bed clad in his T-shirt and boxers.

Sean moved closer, reached up to cup Jeff's cheek. "Goodnight, Tiger," he said softly. "Sleep tight."

"Don't let the bedbugs bite," Jeff said softly.

Sean bent down and hovered his lips over Jeff's for a brief moment, and then Jeff arched up and touched his lips to Sean's. Just a light, sweet kiss, and then they both settled down to sleep.

THE next morning, Sean woke first, aware of Jeff's warmth behind him in the bed and an ache in his groin. He acknowledged again that things had changed and that he was indeed different. It was hard to reconcile that he was waking up with someone he wanted and wasn't taking *what* he wanted. Once the ache subsided down into typical morning wood, he rolled over. The movement of the bed woke Jeff.

"Mornin'," Sean said softly.

Jeff kept his head bent, kept his gaze lowered. "I'm sorry, Sean."

"Sorry?" Sean clenched his fingers into a fist to keep from reaching out and threading them through Jeff's hair, raising his head so their eyes could meet. "Why are you sorry?"

"Because." Jeff paused and took a deep breath. "I should have just gone home yesterday, not bothered you by sleeping here and letting you wake up with me when I know that you want—"

"Don't put words in my mouth, Jeff," Sean murmured.

Jeff tensed and began to slide away, mumbling, "Sorry... so sorry."

The intimacy of lying in bed spurred Sean to reach over and clasp Jeff's arm, holding him from getting up.

"Just one question," he said softly. "What are you so afraid of?"

"I'm afraid of me, Sean," Jeff said, his voice twisted with anguish.

"Listen, Tiger," Sean said, hoping to soothe things with the use of the endearment, "you keep saying you know what I want, and now you're apologizing for things that I don't understand. I told you last night was just to sleep, because of the thunderstorm."

Although he didn't try to pull further away, Jeff didn't shift closer either, and he still kept his eyes averted from Sean.

"What is it that you think I want from you?" Sean whispered. "And why are you afraid of yourself?"

Only then did Jeff look up, and the depth of emotion in his eyes tore at Sean's heart. "You want me, Sean, and I'm afraid because I want you too."

Sean slid closer, moving slowly so that Jeff wouldn't break away and leave the bed. "I do want you, Jeff. I want to make love to you, watch the passion inside your eyes and not the fear I see now. That's why I'll wait until you're ready. I just, I don't understand what's so frightening. You're not a virgin, are you?"

Eyes closed again, Jeff shook his head.

"Then what's the problem? It's just you and me here, Jeff, only the two of us, and I won't judge you for anything you say." Sean released his hold on Jeff's arm to lend credence to his words.

Jeff shivered and burrowed down under the sheet. "I'm not ready yet, Sean. It's too soon after Hunter. I can't"—he paused and twisted his hands together—"I don't want to lose myself again like that, and even though I know you're not like him, there's a part of me that is just messed up."

The chief emotion oozing from Jeff was self-loathing. Sean knew there was more to the story, but he also knew that this was a huge barrier that had been crossed. He still kept his distance, and he said, "Listen, Jeff, I'm not going to push you. I just want you to know that I want a physical relationship with you, but I don't want it to be based on fear, so I'm willing to wait. Until you're ready. And if I ask you to stay again, it will just be to sleep."

A solitary tear leaked from the corner of Jeff's eye, and after a moment, he opened his eyes and looked at Sean. "Okay," he said, and he cleared his throat. "I like staying here."

"Hell, you can move in if you want," Sean said. "I'd like that."

Jeff smiled then, and his voice broke as he said, "We'll see."

Sean eased closer and pressed his lips to the tip of Jeff's nose. "You want the shower first?"

"I better go," Jeff said. "You have to get ready for work and everything."

Not wanting to push him, Sean let Jeff get up and start pulling on his clothes before he got out of the bed himself. "If you move in, though," he said, "then you'll have to get up first so you can make me my breakfast while I shower." He said it playfully.

"Really?" Jeff said. "You'd let me?"

Sean chuckled and said, "I was just teasing you, Jeff." He pulled on a pair of track pants and followed Jeff out of the room.

"Oh," Jeff said, crestfallen. "I'd like to make you breakfast."

"Then the next time you stay, I'll let you," Sean said. "Give you an incentive for staying over again."

Jeff smiled and picked up Dakotah's leash, busying himself with slipping the leash over the dog's head. "I promise, Sean," he said when he stood up. "I'll stay over again soon."

"Good." Sean reached down to pet the dog and then leaned in for another light kiss. "See you later?"

"Yeah," Jeff said, "I'll see you tonight."

Sean watched as Jeff and Dakotah walked out the back way. The rain had gone for the time being, but there was a promise of more rain later. Sean headed down the hall to the bathroom. He had all day to ponder over the stilted conversation with Jeff and puzzle out who this Hunter character was. The more pressing need was to rid himself of this hard-on. A hand job in the shower wasn't really what he wanted, but it would suffice.

For now.

Chapter 6

Gentle Strength

JEFF began staying with Sean every night after that, and after a while, Sean gave him a key to his house. At first Jeff went home every morning and rarely came early enough to let himself in before Sean got home from work. Eventually, they settled into a routine where Jeff stayed at the house most of the time.

Sean mentioned it to Gabriel and withstood the lecture about how he didn't know Jeff that well. Gabriel asked if they were sleeping together, and after Sean growled that it was none of Gabriel's business, he finally acknowledged that he had made it Gabriel's business simply by telling him that Jeff was staying over. After avoiding the question by saying they were indeed *sleeping* with each other, he finally admitted that as of yet there was no sex. Gabriel cautioned Sean to be careful, and Sean took the advice with good grace.

One lazy Saturday afternoon, Sean sat working on a model, and after Jeff had washed the breakfast dishes and put them away, he came in to sit and watch.

"Hey, Tiger," Sean said as he looked up with a smile. "Give me a hand and trim the edges of that next piece for me." He handed Jeff the piece and a small knife.

With shaking hands, Jeff took the piece. "I can't." He looked up at Sean. "I can't use the knife, Sean. It's too sharp."

"That's nonsense," Sean said, and he continued to hold the knife out toward Jeff.

"But," Jeff said, and he faltered.

"Take it, Jeff. It's not as sharp as you think it is," Sean said, cocking his head to the side. He remembered the last time they'd talked about prepping the pieces, and Jeff had balked at using the knife. He knew Jeff was more comfortable with him now, but he suspected he still wasn't ready to tell him why the knife bothered him so much.

Jeff dipped his head and clasped his hands together.

Slowly, Sean got up and came to stand behind Jeff. "Look," he said quietly, "I'll show you how to use the knife so you won't get hurt. Then, if you still don't want to, we'll put the model away until you're ready." He gently pried Jeff's hands apart and put the knife in his palm.

Hesitantly, Jeff tightened his hand around the knife and picked up one of the model pieces. He had watched Sean so many times that he knew what to do. Sean watched as Jeff trimmed the first piece, and he smiled.

"You got it, Jeff, that's the way." He turned to go back to work on his own model.

His hands shaking, Jeff put down the first piece and picked up the next one. This time he nicked the tip of his finger, and tears welled in his eyes. Casting a quick look over his shoulder, he saw that Sean was engrossed in his work, so he put the injured finger into his mouth. After a minute he tried again and nicked another finger. This time, he dropped the knife on the table.

Sean turned at the sound, and when he saw Jeff with his fingers in his mouth, he scooted off his stool and came over. "What happened, Tiger?"

Reluctantly, Jeff pulled his fingers from his mouth. "I cut myself by accident."

"I know it was an accident, Jeff," Sean said. "No one cuts themselves on purpose." He gave a lopsided smile. "Come on, let's get you bandaged up."

Jeff followed him into the kitchen, where Sean washed his cuts and bandaged them up. When he was done, he kissed the bandages and winked. "You can't work like that," he said as he washed his own hands. "I have to run over to the model shop and get some green paint. Want to come along?"

"I better take Dakotah for a walk," Jeff said, his voice quavering as if he were holding back tears.

"Suit yourself," Sean said. He grabbed up his keys. "I'll be back soon."

After Sean left, Jeff wandered out into the back yard. He found Dakotah asleep in the doghouse Sean had built for him. He looked peaceful, and without really thinking about it, Jeff climbed in beside him. "Love you, Kotah," he whispered as the dog resettled against him. Before long they were both asleep.

When Sean returned, he found them there and smiled. He came over and squatted down beside the doghouse, reached in and laid his hand on the back of Jeff's head. "Why are you in the doghouse, Tiger?" he asked.

Jeff's eyes fluttered open, and Dakotah rolled over, his tail thumping against the side of the doghouse.

"I can't sleep, Sean," Jeff said, his voice rough with sleep. "At my house I was scared to sleep alone, and in your bed I get nightmares."

Sean frowned, tightened his grip. "Why do you get nightmares? Am I that frightening?"

"No," Jeff said, and he bit his lip. "It's just that I want you so bad, and my unconscious mind thinks you don't want me back."

Dakotah scampered out of the doghouse, and Sean said with a low growl, "Let me make love to you Jeff, please?" as if all the pieces had finally fallen into place.

Jeff gasped, and he rolled over to hold out his uninjured hand. Sean hauled him out of the doghouse, held his hand, and turned to lead him into the kitchen. They continued through to the bedroom, and once there, Sean pulled Jeff into a tight hug, felt him quivering against him.

"It's okay, Jeff," he said softly. "I do want you, I want you so much, but I didn't want to push you." He cupped Jeff's jaw and raised his head so their eyes could meet. "I was waiting for you to be ready."

Jeff raised his arms and looped them up around Sean's neck. "I want this," he whispered.

With another barely stifled growl, Sean dipped his head and touched his lips to Jeff's. Caution was not in his nature, but he held himself back and moved slowly. The kiss deepened between them, and Sean lowered his hands to cup Jeff's ass, holding him close. When he felt Jeff shiver, he eased them both back toward the bed.

Jeff sat on the edge of the bed and toed his shoes off, watching as Sean removed his jacket and stepped out of his own shoes. He scooted back when Sean joined him.

"You're shaking like a leaf, Jeff," Sean murmured. He skimmed his hand down Jeff's side, leaned in closer to brush his lips over his cheek.

"Because I want you, Sean," Jeff whispered.

"Shh," Sean groaned, and he pressed his lips against Jeff's. He opened his mouth to deepen the kiss, and he slid his hand up under Jeff's shirt.

Jeff mewled softly, one hand gripping the covers below him, the other gripped tightly to Sean's shirt. He returned the kiss eagerly.

Sean pulled back and propped himself up on his elbow. Jeff's eyes were narrowed in desire, his lips bruised from the kiss, his hair tousled across the pillow. "You're so beautiful, Jeff," Sean murmured as he stroked up Jeff's side under his shirt. "Let me see you."

In answer, Jeff raised both arms above his head, and Sean slowly slid his shirt up and off. He bent forward and pressed soft lips against his chest as he trailed his hands down lower and teased against his waistband.

"Let me know, Jeff," Sean said softly as he nuzzled over his flesh, "if I'm moving too fast."

Jeff gasped in answer, lowered his hand to grip at Sean's shoulder again. "Want this," he murmured.

Sean rose up to kiss Jeff again as he slowly worked on unbuttoning his jeans. His own erection swelled painfully within the confines of his jeans, but he focused on holding himself in check. He trailed kisses from Jeff's mouth to the shell of his ear, back down his neck, and finally had Jeff's jeans open. Rather than yank them off, he eased his hand inside, cupped Jeff's erection through the cotton of his boxers. He murmured into Jeff's open mouth, "You feel good."

A hard shiver coursed through Jeff's body. He released his hold and arched up against Sean. Unable to form words, he moaned an invitation.

Sean rose up on his knees and began to slowly ease Jeff out of his jeans, leaving his boxers in place for the time being. In the back of his mind, he reminded himself that Jeff had apparently suffered pain at the hands of his previous lover. The lust in his soul was hard to contain. He sat back and looked down at Jeff as he lay with arms over his head, his boxers tented out with obvious desire.

"Christ, you're sexy," he whispered.

Jeff stretched languidly in open invitation, and Sean eased down against him, kissed him deeply as he slipped his hand under the elastic waistband of Jeff's boxers. Continuing to kiss Jeff, he slid the boxers down and wrapped his hand around his length. Pressing his forehead against Jeff's, his breathing ragged with desire, Sean stroked up Jeff's length and then smeared his precum back down his shaft.

With another wordless moan, Jeff undulated under Sean's touch. Sean rose up to kiss him again, and then, shifting, he pressed kisses over his nipple, his ribcage, and his bellybutton. He released Jeff's erection and pressed his lips against the tip while moving his hands down to grip Jeff's hips.

"Oh, shit," Jeff groaned, and his body went tense.

Sean knew instantly that something had changed, and he rose up on his knees to look at Jeff. His eyes were squeezed shut, and he gripped both hands together over his chest. Sean looked down at Jeff's body, and when he moved his hands, he saw that his hips were both covered in scars. On his left hip there were four scars, each a perfectly formed "H," and on his right hip was just one roughly shaped scar, the letter "J." Not wanting to make the connection in his head between the letter H and the man, Hunter, that Jeff had mentioned, Sean eased down beside Jeff and pulled him close.

"Shh," he soothed. "It's okay, Jeff. I'm here."

"You can't," Jeff said, agony clear in his voice, "can't still want me."

"Hush," Sean murmured. "I want you, Jeff." At a loss, he just held him close, pressing soft kisses to the top of his head.

"But I'm so ugly," Jeff wailed. "How could you want me after you saw how ugly?"

"Stop," Sean crooned. He trailed his hand down and caressed Jeff's hip. "You're not ugly."

Jeff pulled away, but Sean held him tightly. "But you can't want me still," Jeff whimpered.

"I do, Jeff," Sean whispered. "Maybe more now because I want to take away all that pain you have inside you."

"You can't take that away," Jeff said, his voice cracking. "It's always pain, always."

"No," Sean growled, "it doesn't have to be. Let me make love to you, Jeff, and show you there's no pain."

Jeff trembled against Sean but stopped trying to struggle away. His breath came in ragged sobs, but he reached out and gripped at Sean's shoulder again.

"Please," Sean whispered.

As if that was his undoing, Jeff nodded against Sean's chest, and as Sean released his grip, Jeff rolled back down against the bed. Jeff kept his eyes glued to Sean as he began to slowly stroke his body again. "Can I... see you?" he whispered at last.

Sean's grin was almost feral as he sat up and stripped off his shirt. Years of working out had muscled his body. Urgency took over as he popped the buttons of his jeans and yanked them off along with his briefs. He sat back on his haunches to let Jeff look at him and groaned when Jeff reached up to close his hand around his erection.

"So big," Jeff whispered.

"I won't hurt you," Sean said, and he leaned over to slide the drawer of the bedside table open and take out lube and a condom. He eased back down beside Jeff and slid his fingers down over his balls to tease against his opening.

"I know," Jeff said, and he gasped, this time in pleasure, when Sean slid his fingers inside. He widened his legs and raised both arms above his head again.

Sean groaned at the erotic display and eased two fingers inside Jeff's willing body. He kissed Jeff's forehead and groaned again as his erection brushed against Jeff's leg. It was becoming increasingly difficult to hold back.

"Oh God, Sean," Jeff whimpered, "I want—"

Twisting his fingers one last time, Sean rose up on his knees. He reached for the condom, and as Jeff spread himself wider, he dripped more lube down on his puckered hole. Sean held one of Jeff's legs up against his chest, pressed against him, and slowly began to slide inside.

Jeff kept his eyes locked on Sean's face, and he eased up to pull Sean in deeper. He reached up, and Sean bent closer to kiss the tips of his bandaged fingers again as he sank in completely.

For a long moment they were connected, body to body, eye to eye, lips to fingers, and then Jeff's eyes slipped closed, and he spread his arms wide across the bed.

"Touch me, Sean," he moaned.

The spell broken, Sean closed his fist around Jeff's length. He moved inside him slowly, needing to hold out until Jeff came first. His fingers still sticky with lube, he stroked Jeff's length and angled his thrusts to nudge against his spot. Goosebumps raised along his flesh as he watched Jeff's response.

"Feels good, Sean," Jeff moaned. "Feels so good."

"Fuck," Sean gritted. "Come undone for me." He tightened his grip and stroked harder.

Jeff arched up, and with a broken wail, he spilled. "Sean," he whispered, and he opened his eyes a crack, his body flushed with desire.

Sean bit his lower lip, needing to hold out just long enough to take in the tableau of Jeff's body spread before him, the feel of his fluttering passage, and more importantly, his name on Jeff's lips. At last the vision overpowered him, and he let go, pulled back and slammed hard against Jeff's body. It only took one thrust before he broke, and he rolled forward as the orgasm sang through his body.

Careful not to crush Jeff, Sean lowered himself down against the bed and held Jeff close. His body tingled with release, and he could tell by the way that Jeff clung to him that Jeff's body tingled as well. Twisted together, they breathed in one another's scent until at last Sean murmured, "Are you still sleepy?"

Afraid to speak and break the spell, Jeff just nodded.

Sean sat up and peeled the condom off, dropping it onto the wrapper on the bedside table. He yanked the covers out from under them and draped them over their bodies before snuggling up against Jeff again. "Just a little nap," he whispered.

Jeff tucked his head under Sean's chin, and together they drifted into a light doze.

Chapter 7

Discovery

JEFF woke first, and a quick glance at the clock showed they'd only slept for about an hour. He pulled back far enough to study Sean's body, but not so far that they weren't still touching. Although he longed to reach out and touch, he didn't want to wake Sean as he took time to internalize all the feelings that had been awakened inside him.

Before he had the chance, Sean stirred and stretched. He smiled when his leg nudged against Jeff's under the covers, and he opened his eyes. Moving closer, he reached for Jeff's hand and threaded their fingers together. "Hey," he said softly.

"Hey," Jeff said. He shivered and dipped his head.

"You okay?" Sean asked.

"Yeah," Jeff whispered. "Should we get up?"

"Why?" Sean asked. "I'm not in any hurry."

"Feels like we're wasting time," Jeff said.

"This ain't a waste of time Jeff," Sean said. "Not by a long shot." He moved forward to kiss the top of Jeff's head. "We'll get up later, but for right now, I just want to be here. With you."

Jeff shivered and moved in a little closer against Sean's body.

"You okay?" Sean asked again, and he casually dipped his free hand down to brush it over Jeff's ass.

"Yeah," Jeff said. "Would you... tell me a story?"

"A story?" Sean said. "What kind of a story?"

"A story about you," Jeff said.

Sean chuckled. "There's not much to tell about me. I was the bad kid who always got in trouble at school. Somehow I made good enough grades to get me into college, and while I was there, I spent more time hanging out and partying with my friends than studying. Funny thing is, though, all of us ended up going on to make something out of ourselves."

"You went to college?" Jeff said. He pulled back to look at Sean.

Sean grinned. "Yeah, got a degree in history and still managed to get a good job."

"Wow," Jeff said wistfully. "If I could go to college, I'd study history too."

"You could go to college if you wanted," Sean said. "You could do anything you set your mind to, Jeff."

"I never graduated from high school," Jeff said, and he pushed closer again, keeping his face turned away from Sean.

"You can get a GED. I'll help you if you want," Sean said.

"No, it's just…." Jeff hesitated. "I'm too stupid for that, Sean, and I can't even read. That's why I dropped out. I can't read."

Sean propped himself up on an elbow and gently eased Jeff's chin up. "Why can't you read? Do you think you need glasses?"

"I can see the words," Jeff said softly, "but they just move around all over the page, like they can't stay still or something. I just gave up because everyone yelled at me about it and thought I was lazy."

"Have you ever been tested for dyslexia?" Sean asked.

"Dis-what?"

"Dyslexia. I'm not an expert or anything, but that's what happens when people have dyslexia. The letters transpose themselves." Sean lowered himself down again and caressed Jeff's arm gently. "When was the last time you saw a doctor?"

Soft color washed across Jeff's cheeks. "Not for a long time," he lied. He wasn't ready to tell Sean about the recent doctor visits, not yet anyway.

"Well, I have a college buddy who is a doc. In fact, you met him at the park that first time we met each other. Remember him?" Sean said. "His name's Gabe. He's got that wild hair that looks like he stuck his finger in an electric socket."

"I don't remember," Jeff said. "I don't remember a lot about that day, except you."

Sean smiled and put his arm around Jeff and pulled him in close. "Maybe you'll remember when you see him. I'll call him up and see if we can get you an appointment to see him." He nuzzled against the top of Jeff's head.

"I don't really want to see a doctor, Sean," Jeff said.

"It won't hurt to get a checkup," Sean said, and he settled their bodies together. He continued to idly caress Jeff's back.

"Sean?" Jeff said at last, his voice small and muffled against Sean's chest.

"Mmm?" Sean murmured.

"Thank you," Jeff said softly. "For everything."

"You don't have to thank me, Jeff."

"Yeah," Jeff said, "but what if I want to anyway?"

Sean smiled. "Okay, funny business, then you can thank me."

They fell into companionable silence then. There was still time in the day to clean up the workroom and then make dinner. And there would always be time for Sean to begin to unwrap the mysteries of Jeff.

WHEN Sean called Gabriel later in the day, he set up the appointment for the following Monday. Not wanting to burst the bubble of happiness that Sean suspected was making Jeff smile so often, he waited until the next night to tell him about the appointment.

Monday morning, Jeff stood beside Sean nervously in the waiting room of the clinic. He thought he had hidden his fear, but Sean gripped his hand tightly, as if communicating that it was okay to be nervous. In some respects, Jeff was surprised that Sean cared so much, but it only took one touch, one kiss, and Jeff melted inside.

A nurse led them back to an exam room, and Sean said softly, "I'll stay with you, Tiger, if you want."

Jeff gasped. "Please don't leave me, Sean." He sat on the paper-covered exam table, and Sean stood by the counter, arms folded over his chest.

"You're going to be okay, Jeff, don't worry."

Gabriel came into the room and took Sean's hand, pulled him into a hug. They greeted one another while Jeff sat with his hands clasped tightly together in his lap.

"Now do you remember him, Jeff?" Sean asked as he stepped back.

"Yeah," Jeff said, his voice tight with worry.

Gabriel stepped forward and offered his hand. "I'm Dr. Romano, Jeff," he said. "We met in the park."

"Uh huh," Jeff said. He didn't offer his hand to be shaken.

"It's okay, Jeff," Sean said soothingly, exchanging a look with Gabriel.

"Sean tells me you're having a little trouble with reading," Gabriel said, his voice warm. "Tell you what. I want to make a full exam. Why don't you strip down to your shorts?" He turned and took a soft cotton gown from a drawer. "Put this on, and I'll be right back." He stepped into the hallway and closed the door behind him.

"What's wrong, Tiger?" Sean said as he helped Jeff with his clothes.

"I don't like doctors, Sean. They scare me," Jeff mumbled.

"Try to relax," Sean said. "Gabriel's not like most doctors."

Just then there was a knock on the door, and Gabriel stepped back into the room. "All ready?" He set Jeff's chart down on the counter and then stepped closer. "How long has it been since you've seen a doctor?"

Jeff hunched forward, his hands back together in his lap. "A long time," he mumbled.

"Well," Gabriel said softly, "I want to listen to your heart and lungs, take your blood pressure, look into your ears, and take some blood. Sound okay?"

Jeff nodded; Sean could feel the tension radiating off him across the room as he sat by the wall. "Take it easy, Jeff," he said softly.

Gabriel took the stethoscope from around his neck and rubbed it against the front of his lab coat to warm it. "Tell me about reading, Jeff," he said softly. "How long have you had trouble with it?"

"Forever," Jeff mumbled.

"What happens?" Gabriel asked. He listened to Jeff's heart and lungs.

"The words jump around on the page," Jeff said softly, "and switch places and stuff. Smaller words I can figure out, but the big ones just confuse me."

As soon as Gabriel took the stethoscope from his ears, Jeff shrank back away from him. Gabriel frowned and picked up the blood pressure cuff. He noticed that Jeff closed his eyes as he put it on him.

"Well, let me ask you this," Gabriel said as he began to pump up the cuff. "Do you ever lose your balance? Do you fall down easily?"

"Yeah," Jeff said, his face a mask of misery. "I'm a klutz."

Gabriel recorded Jeff's blood pressure, then picked up the instrument to check his ears. "I doubt you're a klutz. Sometimes a lack of balance is a sign of dyslexia," he said with a smile. "I'm going to look in your ears now, okay?"

Jeff nodded, and Sean saw him suppress a shiver as Gabriel brushed his hair aside and looked into his ears. He scooted close enough to reach over and take his hand.

When he was done, Gabriel turned aside and went over to write in Jeff's chart. Jeff kept his head bent. He didn't make eye contact with Sean, but he didn't pull away either.

"It's entirely possible that you are dyslexic, Jeff," Gabriel said, keeping his back to them. "I'd like to run some tests here at the clinic and then have you make an appointment with an eye doctor. You might need glasses." He turned then, a smile on his face. "In the meantime, I'm going to give you some vitamins to try. They might help you with your balance problem. Now, don't get dressed yet, I need to send Karen in to get some blood. Before you leave, stop by the front desk to get your appointment for the tests."

Jeff nodded, but he didn't look up to make eye contact.

"I'll wait out front," Gabriel said.

"Sure thing," Sean replied.

Gabriel stepped out into the hallway, and Sean stood, put his hand on Jeff's shoulder. "I don't get it, Jeff," he said. "I know doctors are scary, but Gabe's a friend. He shouldn't be as scary as a regular doctor."

"He's your friend, Sean," Jeff said. "I don't know him very well."

There was a knock at the door, and Karen came in to take the blood sample. When she was done, she told them Jeff could get dressed and that the paperwork for the tests and the vitamins were waiting at the front desk. After she left, Sean began to pick up Jeff's clothes.

"I'd like for you to think of Gabe as your friend too someday, Jeff. He's my best friend, and he's a great guy."

"Maybe," Jeff said, and taking a deep breath, he said, "I just have a hard time trusting men I don't know very well."

"No pressure," Sean said with a lopsided smile.

Gabriel was waiting with the paperwork and vitamins at the front desk.

"Here you go, Jeff," Gabe said. "This is a B-vitamin. I'd like you to start taking it once a day, either before bed or with your breakfast. Within a month or so, it should start helping you feel more balanced. Here's the card for an eye doctor I recommend, and here's the appointment card for your lab tests. After that, I'll make another appointment for you to see me because I'll want to discuss the results of the tests with you."

Jeff took the vitamins and handed the paperwork over to Sean. He kept his eyes averted from Gabriel and mumbled, "Thanks."

"We'll get you taken care of, Jeff," Gabriel said. "Dyslexia is a problem that can be brought under control. Don't look so frightened. You're in good hands with this big lug." Gabriel turned and punched Sean playfully on the arm. They both laughed, and Jeff hunched his shoulders.

Jeff was quiet on the drive home, and Sean didn't want to stir things up by pushing him. Finally, to break the silence, he said, "Penny for your thoughts?"

"There's a lot of stuff I need to tell you, Sean," Jeff said at last with a sigh.

"Take your time, Jeff," Sean said, and he took one hand off the wheel to reach over and cover Jeff's hands in his lap. "I'm not going anywhere."

Jeff unclasped his hands and laid one of his hands over Sean's.

Chapter 8

A Little Bit

SEAN came home one night the next week to find the house dark. A frown puckered his brow as he parked the car, hoping that Jeff hadn't fled back to Jesse's house. Dakotah greeted him at the fence, and Sean took that as a good sign. He walked up the steps to the back door, went through the kitchen, and detected a flickering glow in the living room.

"Jeff?" he said softly. He rounded the corner and gasped. A fat, warmly spiced candle burned on the coffee table. Next to it sat a huge vase filled with roses and daisies. Jeff was curled in Sean's favorite chair.

Jeff smiled and stood, seemed to almost glide over to step into Sean's embrace. He whispered against Sean's chest, "Missed you."

Sean tightened the hug and said, "I always miss you, Tiger."

"Remember when I said I had some things to tell you?" Jeff murmured.

"I remember," Sean said.

"I think I'm ready to tell you now," Jeff said. "But I don't know where to start."

Sean stepped back and tipped Jeff's chin up. "I think it's always best to start at the beginning," he said with a small smile.

Jeff turned and led Sean back to the chair, and once he was seated, Jeff sat on the floor beside him and leaned in against his leg.

"When I was small, I was convinced my parents didn't want me. Who would? I was always in trouble at school, and I was ugly and a klutz."

Sean couldn't see Jeff's face, but he imagined that he had drifted off, locked in the memories of his childhood. He listened as Jeff recounted his story and didn't interrupt.

"Mom and Dad were killed in a car wreck when I was thirteen and Luke was sixteen. We went to live with Jesse because he was their best friend. He didn't want us. I knew that right away. He tolerated Luke because he was smart and graduated with honors; I was just a burden. So after Luke moved away for college, I dropped out of school, stopped coming home anymore. Jesse didn't even come after me, like he was relieved or something."

Sean reached down and laid his hand on the back of Jeff's head in a soothing caress.

"I started hanging out with my friends on the streets. Some of the guys turned tricks for money, but even though I always knew I was gay, I wouldn't do that. I just played the pathetic waif, and people would give me money just so I'd get out of their sight. Then, one night, we ended up at this club. One of my friends sucked off the bouncer in the alley, and he let us in. That's where I met Hunter."

Biting his lip, Sean eased his hand back, afraid he would tighten it in Jeff's hair as he listened to this talk about the man he knew had hurt Jeff.

"He told me I was pretty. He bought me some drinks, gave me some money, and told me to come back the next day. I did, and before too long, he took me out to his car and said I was so pretty he wanted to see all of me." Jeff paused and then took a deep breath. "He blew my mind that night, best fucking blowjob I've ever gotten. The next night he asked me to come home with him, and I did."

The candle sputtered, breaking the mood for a moment.

"In the beginning it was amazing: he bought me clothes, took me places, and treated me like I was the best thing in the world. I believed him when he told me I was beautiful. We went to the club, and he showed me off like I was his prized possession." Jeff turned to meet Sean's gaze. "One night when we were there, I saw some guy that kept looking at me, and I kept looking at him. When Hunter saw, he got really pissed and accused me of making eyes at the guy behind his back. He dragged me out of there by my hair, took me back home, and that's the first time he cut me."

Stifling a growl, Sean reached down and hauled Jeff up into his lap. He wrapped both arms around him and held him close.

"Do you want me to stop?" Jeff whispered.

Sean took a deep breath. "No, I just need to hold you."

"Hunter told me he wanted me to remember who I belonged to, so that's why he cut an H into my hip. It wasn't the knife that hurt so much. It was so sharp, I barely felt it. He poured vinegar on it after because he said it made the scar set. That burned like fire. Then he forced me down on my knees, and when he fucked me he tore me up, like he enjoyed hurting me."

Sean wrapped his arms more tightly around Jeff.

"After that, he didn't take me out anymore, just kept me like a prisoner at his place. Every time he cut another H, I lost more of myself until I wasn't me anymore."

"Oh, Jeff," Sean whispered, his lips pressed against the top of Jeff's head.

Jeff struggled against Sean's grip and propelled himself out of the chair. He stood shaking for a moment, and then he said, "I have something in my eye," and fled into the bathroom.

Sean remained in the chair, giving Jeff his space as he tried to digest all that Jeff had said. He filled in the blanks and knew that Jeff had been this man Hunter's pet. Although Sean had had a wild past, he had never felt the need to exert power over someone in that way.

Jeff did not return, and at last Sean got up and found the bathroom door closed. He needed to give Jeff his privacy, needed to show Jeff that he respected him. But when he caught the sound of a stifled sob, he leaned in against the door. "Jeff?" he said.

There was no response, and the need to ensure Jeff was okay overrode the need to give him personal space. Sean opened the door and found Jeff kneeling on the floor, a bath towel pressed up against his face to stifle the sound of his crying.

Without a word, Sean dropped to his knees and pulled Jeff into his lap. At first he struggled away, and Sean whispered, "Shh, Jeff, it's me… Sean."

"I'm sorry," Jeff wailed. "Sorry."

"Hush, Tiger," Sean said, deliberately using the pet name to help Jeff differentiate between past and present. "You don't need to be sorry."

Jeff pressed the towel against his face again and mumbled, "I know you don't want to see me cry, I know I'm not strong, I know everything's my fault."

"Stop, Jeff," Sean said. "Nothing's your fault. It's okay to cry sometimes."

Shaking his head, Jeff continued to mumble that everything was his fault.

Sean pried the towel out of Jeff's hands and cupped his face between both of his hands. "Jeff, you're a lot stronger than most people would have been in that situation. What he did to you was wrong."

Jeff shuddered, and his crying eased, but he kept his eyes closed and his face averted from Sean.

Sean stood, pulling Jeff along with him, stepped into the tub, and eased them both down. He cradled Jeff against him, tucked him in close against his body, and gave the illusion that they were locked safely away from the world. After a while, Jeff began to talk again, so softly Sean hardly heard him.

"I ran away from him one night, after he passed out. I didn't know where to go, so I went back to Jesse's. I didn't really want to see him, but I just didn't have any other place to go. I knew what I had to do, but I just didn't know how to do it." He took a deep, shuddering breath and said, "I had to get me back. I sat out in his yard under a tree and got high until I figured out how to do it."

Nuzzling against the top of his head, Sean stroked Jeff's back and listened.

"I snuck into the house and got a knife. I was so high I barely knew what I was doing. I watched Hunter cut me so many times I thought I knew what to do, but I didn't. I cut that J way too deep." Jeff shivered. "I almost killed myself."

"But you didn't, Jeff. You didn't," Sean said forcefully.

"I wanted to, though," Jeff said, and he turned in Sean's arms to lay his cheek against his chest. "I always wished I had died that night. Until I met you."

"Shh," Sean crooned. "I've got you, Jeff."

They remained in the tub until it became too uncomfortable, and then Sean led Jeff into the bedroom, where they stripped and rolled under the covers. Spent by his revelation, Jeff went straight to sleep while Sean remained awake digesting all that Jeff had said. Eventually he drifted into a fitful sleep, and when he awoke the next morning, he found himself alone.

Fearing that Jeff had fled, he rolled out of bed and padded barefoot to the living room. There he found Jeff curled up on the couch, one of the daisies from the vase in his hands. He was intent upon the daisy and didn't hear Sean come into the room. Sean watched as Jeff pulled the petals from the flower, and he stepped forward and whispered, "He loves me. He loves me not."

Jeff gasped and looked up at Sean. "How did you know that was what I was doing?"

"Because." Sean eased himself down beside Jeff on the couch. "I was reading your sweet lips." He bent forward and touched his lips to Jeff's, and when Jeff didn't pull away, he pulled Jeff in close beside him.

"Sean," Jeff said, whispering against Sean's mouth, "do you really still want me... even after what I told you last night?"

"Jeff," Sean said as he reached up and threaded his fingers through Jeff's hair, "you're the most beautiful creature I know. You can't see it, and that's what makes it so. If anything, what you told me last night just makes me want you even more."

Jeff shivered and dropping the daisy stem on the carpet. He moved in closer and skimmed his hand over Sean's arm.

"If I have to tell you that every day for the rest of your life," Sean murmured, "then I will, because you excite me." He slipped his hand under the edge of Jeff's shirt. "You intrigue me. You fascinate me."

With a moan, Jeff twisted around to mold himself more tightly to Sean's body. He raised his arms and twined them around Sean's neck.

Sean reached for a handful of roses, crushed them in his palm, and scattered them across the couch. He eased Jeff back down against the scattered rose petals, looming over him for a moment, then bent down over him to kiss him. He shivered when Jeff reached up and skimmed his fingers under his shirt and up his back. He shifted, letting Jeff feel his erection through their loose clothing, and then he whispered, "You arouse me."

Jeff shuddered and arched up.

"Let me fill you, Jeff," Sean whispered. "Please."

"Yes," Jeff moaned.

Accustomed to moving slowly now, Sean stripped the clothes from both their bodies. He stroked Jeff's flesh and bent down to nip at his lips. "I promise," he murmured, "that I won't hurt you."

"Even if it hurts," Jeff whispered, "it won't hurt, not with you, Sean." He reached up and closed his hand around Sean's dripping length. "You make me feel so good."

With a stifled growl, Sean pulled away. He stood looking down at Jeff, his eyes burning with need and desire, and then he turned and stalked into the bedroom, returning with lube and a condom. He settled back between Jeff's widespread legs and leaned forward to press his lips against the head of Jeff's cock.

"Oh!" Jeff arched up and wailed at the sensation.

"Easy," Sean urged. He leaned up to flutter his lips over Jeff's chest as he opened the lube and slicked his fingers. As he slid two fingers inside Jeff's passage, he pressed the flat of his tongue against his nipple, rubbed his thumb gently over Jeff's balls.

Jeff curled up and kissed the top of Sean's head, spreading his legs wider. He shivered at the way Sean took the time to prepare him and arouse him slowly. "I want you," he whispered.

"I know," Sean murmured against his chest. "I can feel it." He twisted his fingers and slid them in deeper, then eased up and nuzzled against Jeff's neck. Their cocks nestled together as Sean continued to gently prepare Jeff's body.

Keeping his fingers lodged inside Jeff's passage, Sean rose up and reached for the condom packet. He tore it open with his teeth, and Jeff reached up to take the condom from him. As Jeff rolled it over Sean's length, he groaned and slowly slipped his fingers free. He lined up and pushed in slowly.

Jeff arched up, kept his eyes open as he watched Sean's face. He gasped as the light from the window bathed Sean's face. He reached up, and Sean bent forward to kiss the tips of his fingers.

"You feel good, Sean," Jeff whispered.

"So do you, Tiger," Sean murmured. He caught Jeff's hand and held it against his chest, pulled out and pushed in again, kept up the rhythm until Jeff finally closed his eyes. Keeping Jeff's hand caged against his chest, he reached down with his other hand and stroked him as he picked up the pace. "Come for me, Jeff," he whispered.

Jeff's eyes opened a crack, and he gasped, arched up, and came with a prolonged wail. Only then did Sean release his hold on Jeff. He thrust in one last time and came as he moaned Jeff's name.

Settling down beside him on the couch again, Sean reached down to retrieve the daisy stem. There was one petal left, and he held it up above them.

"Remember where you were?" he whispered.

Jeff reached up, took hold of the petal, and whispered, "He loves me."

Sean turned and nuzzled against Jeff's cheek. "I do love you."

Jeff shivered and turned to nuzzle against Sean, whispered almost too low to be heard, "I love you, too, Sean."

Chapter 9

Breaking the Code

THE small square of paper was propped up on the kitchen table. Jeff looked at it as he put away the groceries, and when he was done, he sat down and picked it up. It was a note, and as he squinted at it, he realized it was a note for him. Beyond that, he couldn't read it.

Carefully, he spread it out on the table and traced the words with his fingertips. Jeff guessed that Sean had come home while he was out at the grocery store to try once again to talk him into going out to dinner with Gabriel and Mark. Jeff still felt uncomfortable around strange men, and while he had begun to feel comfortable with Gabriel, he had not met Mark yet. He wasn't proud of the fact that he had lied to Sean and told him he didn't feel well. Lying was wrong, but it was better than the alternative of spending time with people he didn't know very well.

The longer he stared at the note, the more distressed he became, until at last a tear dropped on to the page, smearing the word at the bottom. With a gasp, he pushed the note aside and stood up in agitation.

Jeff knew that Sean loved him. The thought was still new in his head and still filled him with a tingling sensation. If he closed his eyes when he thought it, he could still see Sean's face, flushed with orgasm as he said the words. Jeff knew that if he wanted to be worthy of Sean's love, he needed to stop crying over notes and learn how to read them. He had already taken the first step by going to the clinic for the series of tests Gabriel had ordered, and he knew the next step was to make the appointment with the eye doctor.

Before he could chicken out, he dug the card out of the kitchen drawer and pulled the phone close. He closed his eyes once, then opened them again, willing the numbers on the card to stand still. The phone in Sean's kitchen was a sleek new one with lighted numbers. Biting his lip, Jeff squinted from the card to the phone and entered a series of numbers. An angry voice informed him he had a wrong number.

Setting the phone on the table, Jeff gave in to a wave of helplessness. He should have known better. In the past, the only way he could ever make phone calls was when someone programmed the numbers on speed dial for him. Helplessness gave way to anger, and he pushed back from the table, leaving the note and the card where they were.

Faced with spending the whole evening alone, he wasn't sure what he wanted to do. He didn't feel comfortable in Sean's battle room without him there. Restless, he sat down in Sean's chair and picked up his sketchbook but found he didn't have the concentration to draw. Anger and helplessness drained from him, leaving him feeling tired.

At last, with a sigh of irritation, he went and undressed, then flung himself on the bed. Before long, he drifted into a fitful sleep, as if the lie that he didn't feel well were becoming the truth.

On the other side of town, Sean enjoyed his dinner with Gabriel and Mark. It was like old times, the three of them spending the night drinking and telling stories. Mark was curious to meet Jeff, teasing that both Sean and Gabriel spoke so highly of him Mark wanted to see if he indeed could walk on water. Sean shot back that he was curious to meet the mysterious Todd, and with a flushed face, Mark changed the subject.

Sean begged off at midnight, saying that he needed to go home and check on Jeff. Although he knew that Jeff hadn't been honest about not feeling well, he had let the lie stand because he knew that Jeff was still making baby steps to overcome his past. He suffered the good-natured teasing of Gabriel and Mark and was home within half an hour.

Jeff was asleep, curled into a ball on his side, his cheeks flushed and his lips moving as if he were having a nightmare. Sean dropped down beside him and laid a hand on his cheek, concerned that Jeff was indeed sick. There had been times when Jeff suffered from nightmares, and although he didn't say, Sean suspected they were nightmares about Hunter. He felt himself tense until Jeff called out softly. "No... no glasses."

Sean moved down and drew Jeff into his arms. "Hush, Tiger," he crooned.

Jeff struggled until he woke up and found it was Sean holding him. Then he relaxed and buried his face against Sean's chest.

"What happened? What were you dreaming about?" Sean asked.

After a prolonged silence, Jeff whispered, "I tried to make an appointment with the eye doctor."

Running a thumb along Jeff's cheek, Sean moved closer and kissed him lightly. "You tried?"

"I got a wrong number," Jeff said. "I don't know how—" He sighed and said, "I have a hard time pushing the right numbers."

"Oh, Tiger," Sean said as he brushed the hair away from Jeff's face, "I can make the appointment for you, as long as you're ready for it now." He kissed Jeff's brow and murmured, "What made you decide you're ready?"

Jeff blinked. His eyes were large and luminous in the dark. "It was your fault."

Sean rolled back. "My fault?" He smiled. "How is it my fault?"

Jeff scooted to the side of the bed and stood. Silently, he walked from the room and came back with the note. He climbed back up in bed and handed it over. "I couldn't read it."

Scooting up to lean back against the headboard, Sean looked at the note he'd casually written that afternoon. He reached over to turn on the bedside light and noticed the smudge where Jeff's tear had fallen. He bit his lip, realizing that when he had written the note, he hadn't even thought about the fact that Jeff wouldn't be able to read it.

"What does it say?" Jeff asked as he snuggled in along Sean's side.

"Just that I love you and that I wouldn't be back late," Sean murmured.

Jeff sighed and forlornly rested his head on Sean's chest. "I want to be able to read what you write, Sean, especially if you say you love me."

Sean kissed the top of Jeff's head and whispered, "If that's what it takes, Jeff, then I'll write you a note every day."

Jeff reached over and took the note. "Which word says 'love'?"

Taking Jeff's hand in his, Sean pointed out the word, and together they traced it with their fingers. Then Jeff rose up and shifted himself so that he was half atop Sean. He bent down and kissed him.

Shivering with the intensity of the knowledge that Jeff was initiating contact for the first time, Sean willed himself to hold back and let Jeff set the pace. The kiss was sweet and fueled with a need that Jeff was still timid about unleashing. Sean reached up and tangled his fingers through Jeff's hair.

"Let me have you," he whispered.

"Oh, Sean," Jeff moaned, "you can have me any time you want without asking."

"I know," Sean murmured, "but I think you like it when I ask."

Jeff rolled off Sean's body and reached down to slip his boxers off. He watched as Sean stood and stripped out of his jeans and T-shirt, set lube and a condom on the bedside table, and then eased back in beside him again.

Sean smoothed the hair out of Jeff's eyes and then bent in for a kiss. Jeff moaned up into his mouth and ran his hands over Sean's arms. Breaking the kiss, Sean eased down and kissed the pulse in Jeff's neck. He trailed his hand down as he kissed slowly down the length of Jeff's body.

Moaning and raising his arms above his head, Jeff arched up into each kiss. He tipped his head to the side to watch as Sean tongued over a nipple and then nipped down the center of his chest until he pressed his lips against Jeff's belly button. Jeff spread his legs to let Sean settle between them and gasped as Sean moved over to lovingly kiss each scar on his hip.

"Sean," Jeff moaned, "it feels so good when...." He couldn't finish the thought, as he was assaulted by the knowledge that each time Sean kissed him this way he took away a little more of his pain.

Sean eased back to meet Jeff's gaze, and then he eased over and kept his eyes locked on Jeff's as he flicked his tongue across the head of Jeff's cock.

"Oh." Jeff squeezed his eyes shut and gripped both hands into the sheets below him.

Tongue, lips, and tight suction, Sean worked down to the base of Jeff's length and up to the tip. He eased a hand under the back of Jeff's leg and urged it up, spreading his body out to allow for gentle fingering of his hole. Taking Jeff down into his throat, he hummed softly, felt the spasm chase through him. Without dislodging him, Sean reached for the lube and eased one slick finger into Jeff's passage, satisfied with the fluttering feeling that gripped him.

A little of the wild impatience overtook Sean, and he continued the blowjob as he teased his finger deeper, feeling each jump of Jeff's cock when he nudged against his spot. He added another finger as he scraped Jeff's length lightly with his teeth, and when Jeff groaned louder, he slid a third finger inside. At last he pulled up, fingers lodged in Jeff's passage, his lips pressed against the tip of his cock. Sean angled his head back and waited for Jeff to open his eyes again. Only then did he rise up with a nearly feral grin. He reached for the condom and handed it to Jeff, shifting to give Jeff room to maneuver.

With clumsy fingers, Jeff tore open the package, and he curled up to press the condom down over Sean's length, cupped his hands under Sean's sack, and then leaned forward to brush his lips over his chest before flopping back down on the bed.

Easing his fingers free, Sean lifted both of Jeff's legs and settled against his body. He turned to press a soft kiss against Jeff's knee and then began to slide into the tight warmth of his passage.

Jeff's eyes fluttered closed, and then he opened them again, kept them locked on Sean as he moved above him.

"Touch yourself, Tiger," Sean murmured.

Leaving one arm flung above his head, Jeff curled his hand around his length. Each time Sean shoved inside his body, he stroked up.

Sean alternated between looking into Jeff's eyes and watching him stroke his erection. "So fucking good," he murmured at last.

"Can't last," Jeff gasped.

"Then come for me," Sean urged. He pulled back and slammed in hard with a growl, signaling that he couldn't last much longer either.

Jeff came first, his body arching up off the bed with the force of the orgasm. His inner passage gripped tightly around Sean's length and pulled the release from him as well.

Eyes closed, they both rode out their orgasms and tumbled together into a tangle of arms and legs.

"Love you," Jeff whispered when his breathing finally returned to normal.

"Love you back," Sean murmured.

Chapter 10

Cleansing the Soul

THE next day, Sean called and made the appointment for Jeff with the eye doctor. The visit was uneventful aside from the fact that he was indeed prescribed a pair of glasses. Together with Sean, he chose a pair of frames that would not "swallow his whole face," as his nightmare had suggested. On the way home they had ice cream, and Jeff finally convinced Sean to allow him to fix dinner.

"Tomorrow night!" Jeff said excitedly. "I'll go to the market and pick it all out!"

Sean tossed the plastic spoon back into the paper ice cream bowl and smiled. "If I had known it was this easy to get you this worked up, I'd have let you make dinner before."

Jeff chuckled. "Jesse never let me near the kitchen except to pour out cereal and milk." He didn't add a reminder about the knife, but it was clear that was the primary reason Jeff had never been allowed to fix food. "I've been wanting to try cooking a meal forever."

Sean stood and reached for Jeff's hand. "Well, my stomach will be glad to let you try."

Because Jeff didn't drive, it was fortunate that Sean's house was in an area of town where everything Jeff needed was a short walk away. Late in the afternoon the next day, Jeff returned from the market with several bags of groceries.

"Jeff? What's keeping you?"

"Be right there," Jeff replied, and he closed the refrigerator, a satisfied smile on his face. He folded the bags and set them on the counter by the door, then went to find Sean.

Sean sat staring intently at the battle map he was creating on his computer; he turned long enough to raise his head for Jeff's kiss. When he turned back, he said casually, "There's a message for you."

"Me?" Jeff said. "Who would call me?"

Sean grinned and turned back to his computer. "Only one way to find out."

Jeff gingerly pushed the button, and Gabriel's businesslike voice issued from the machine. "This is a message for Jeff. This is Dr. Romano, and your test results have come in. I'd like you to call me as soon as you can so we can schedule an appointment to discuss them. Please call my office, and we'll set it up."

As he listened to the message, Jeff gripped his hands together once again. Sean noticed he did that every time he felt nervous. He reached over and gently pried Jeff's hands apart. "Don't be nervous, Tiger," he said softly. "Whatever he has to tell you, I'll be there to support you."

"But you already know, don't you?" Jeff said.

Sean shook his head. "Why would I already know?"

"Because Dr. Romano is your friend, and I'm sure he already told you."

After a silence, Sean scooted back his chair and pulled Jeff down into his lap. "This is something that is between you and Gabe, Jeff," he said softly. "You are an individual, not a possession. Your medical history belongs to you."

Jeff shivered and said in a small voice, "Will you go with me?"

"I'll take you over there, but I want you to start taking responsibility for yourself. If you get overwhelmed, then I'm sure Gabe will let me come in and sit with you, but I think you're brave enough to do this on your own."

Jeff held Sean's hand and watched as he dialed Gabriel's number. He was surprised to find they had an appointment available that very afternoon. Sean saved his map, and they drove over to the clinic.

When they arrived, Sean stayed in the waiting room with a magazine while Jeff followed the nurse down the hall to Gabriel's office. She showed him in and said that Dr. Romano would be with him soon. Jeff gripped his hands together in his lap, and after a moment or two of nervousness, he began to look around the office. There were pictures on the wall, some certificates behind glass, and a miniature aquarium on the desk. Jeff leaned forward to look at it and caught sight of a plaque resting in a little stand on the desk. He bent closer and squinted at it, unable to read it.

"'A relationship can be wonderful.'"

Startled, Jeff turned to find Gabriel standing just inside the door with a smile on his face as he recited the saying on the plaque from memory.

"'It can also be awful. It can be something—or nothing. But it should never be everything. The single most important relationship in your life should be the one you have with yourself. Love and respect *you*, and the rest will follow.' Hello, Jeff," Gabriel said as he extended his hand. "How are you feeling today?"

"Fine," Jeff said, and after a moment, he reached up to shake his hand.

"I liked the quotation," Gabriel said briskly as he rounded his desk and picked up a clipboard from the credenza behind it. "Liked it enough to have it made into a plaque."

"It's nice," Jeff said nervously as he sank back into his chair.

"We can have Sean come and join us if it would make you feel more comfortable," Gabriel said as he rounded the desk and took the chair next to Jeff.

Jeff shook his head, hearing Sean's voice in his head again telling him to be brave.

"Okay, well we'll call him in later, then." Gabriel smiled at Jeff. "I want you to be comfortable." He reached over for a pen.

Jeff watched as Gabriel settled back in his chair. Although the lab tests had been administered by a technician, Gabriel had been present. This was the third time Jeff had had contact with him, and slowly he was beginning to see that what Sean said was the truth. Gabriel was a doctor, but there really wasn't anything about him that was frightening.

"There were three tests administered," Gabriel said as he settled back in his chair and flipped through the pages on the clipboard. "The first one was called an ENG test, and the good news is that it showed that your inner ear is not abnormal, thus it is not the cause of your loss of balance."

Jeff nodded and flashed on a memory of the day he had come to the clinic with Sean. He had begged to have Sean stay with him during the testing, and when the lab technician had said no, Jeff had been afraid that Sean would knock the technician down, so he had been allowed to stay.

"The posturography test showed that the vitamins are helping your balance, but that it's not completely normal yet. It also showed that there's nothing else wrong with you." He paused and looked over at Jeff. "What I mean by that is that these balance problems are not related to some other kind of illness. They seem to be strictly related to your dyslexia."

"So," Jeff said, his voice a croak from nervousness, "that's what I have, then?"

Gabriel nodded and smiled. "Yes, you are dyslexic, Jeff." He turned the final page on the clipboard and turned it to show it to Jeff. "These are the results from the optokinetic testing. Remember that one? The elephants chasing each other?"

Jeff grimaced as he nodded, remembering that he had lied to the technician when the elephants had blurred as soon as he switched the machine on. Knowing that no one would believe him, he had waited a moment before reporting that the elephants were blurred. The technician had repeated the test several times until Jeff had fallen into a frustrated silence that indicated his difficulty with the test.

"The purpose for the test is to see if your eyes can keep up with the changing speed of the pattern, and your 'blur-out' speed definitely indicates dyslexia. It's a shame it wasn't caught when you were younger, would have saved you a lot of grief."

"I don't know who would have caught it," Jeff mumbled under his breath.

"Teachers. Your parents." Gabriel set the clipboard aside on his desk. "Any number of people could have caught it, Jeff, even you yourself."

"Me?" Jeff snorted and slouched lower in his chair. "How could I have caught it? Any time I tried to tell anyone that the words were moving on the page they'd yell at me, tell me I was lazy." He stopped and swallowed. "Everyone thought I was lying."

"Jeff," Gabriel said, and he leaned over to lay his hand on Jeff's arm, "all those days are in the past, and our primary goal now is to take care of the dyslexia. It will just take a little work and effort. We'll set you up with a tutor."

Jeff sat in silence, absorbing what Gabriel had said, and he slumped down in his chair when Gabriel removed his hand.

"Listen," Gabriel said as he cocked his head to the side, "you seem nervous when you're here. Why is that?"

"You're a doctor. Who wouldn't be nervous?" Jeff mumbled.

"Your nervousness goes beyond that, though," Gabriel said softly. "You seem physically afraid of me."

Jeff gripped the arms of the chair more tightly and finally said, "I am."

"Why?" Gabriel asked, and he watched as Jeff seemed to struggle with an answer. He leaned forward again and said, "Sean and I have been friends for a long time, Jeff, and I can tell you mean a lot to him. No one can force you to choose your friends, but I'd like it if you and I became friends."

"Did Sean tell you about Hunter?" Jeff murmured.

"Not all the details," Gabriel said.

Jeff looked down at his hands, and then very softly he said, "Hunter wasn't a very nice person, Dr. Romano. Before I met him, I thought I could trust everyone, but now...." He looked up, and his voice cracked as he said, "Sometimes I'm just afraid of men I don't know very well."

Gabriel set the clipboard on the edge of his desk. "I'm not going to push you, Jeff, and I won't lie to you and say I understand what you're going through. Sometimes it takes a while to trust people again. Sean gave you the time you needed, and I will too."

Jeff looked up through the fringe of his hair and smiled. "Thank you. I haven't—" He drew a deep breath and said, "It's been a long time since I've had a friend."

Gabriel smiled. "Sean says you don't drive. Do you know how to get here on the bus?"

"Yeah," Jeff said with a smile. "I can't read, but I memorized which bus to take. This place isn't far from this art store I used to go to when I was living on the street. The owner there gave me old sketchbooks. I know this is the stop before his store."

"Then you can come by any time you feel like you need a friend to talk to." Gabriel glanced at the plaque on his desk and said, "Just keep in mind, Jeff, I know you love and respect Sean, but you have to love and respect yourself too."

"It's hard," Jeff said.

"It doesn't have to be," Gabriel said. He stood. "If you don't mind, I'd like to call Sean in so we can go over the results of the blood tests."

Jeff dipped his head in acquiescence, and Gabriel stepped to the door of his office. After a few moments, Sean came in to sit down beside Jeff while Gabriel rounded the desk to sit behind it.

Jeff reached over for Sean's hand and squeezed it. He smiled and said, "I'm not stupid, Sean. You were right—I'm just dyslexic."

Sean twisted in the chair, laid his forehead against Jeff's, and whispered, "I knew you weren't stupid, Tiger."

"He can get past the dyslexia with determination," Gabriel said. "I know a couple of tutors in the area. I'll give you the information."

"Whatever he needs, Sean said.

"One thing you can do to help him with his balance is to take him to the park and play basketball or some other sport. That will also help with his confidence."

"All over that," Sean said with a wink.

"Aside from testing for dyslexia, we also did some blood work, as you recall," Gabriel said as he opened Jeff's chart again. "Bear in mind as we go over these results that I'm not just your friend, Sean, I'm also your doctor."

Sean growled. "I know that."

"The results of HIV testing were negative," Gabriel said, and he raised his head and looked at Jeff. "That means you are not HIV positive." He turned and looked at Sean. "Are you two physically intimate?"

A blush bloomed over Jeff's cheeks, and he tried to pull his hand away from Sean.

Sean turned and murmured to Jeff, "That's why he reminded us he's a doctor, Tiger. If he were just our friend, we'd tell him to fuck off." He turned back and looked at Gabriel. "Yeah, Gabe, we are."

Gabriel smiled gently and said, "This next question is going to be difficult, Jeff, but I need to ask." He paused and took a deep breath. "We talked about Hunter earlier, and from what you said, I gather you were also intimate with him."

Jeff gripped Sean's hand even tighter and simply nodded his head.

"How long has it been since you last had intercourse with him?" Gabriel asked.

"Fuck," Sean muttered. He glared at Gabriel, then bent closer to speak softly to Jeff. "I wish there were some other way, Jeff, but Gabe's not trying to embarrass you or make you feel bad. He just has to know. I know the memory hurts, but when was the last time?"

Gabriel bit his lower lip as he observed Jeff's pain. "How long has he been with you, Sean?" he asked.

Sean frowned as he thought back over the time and then said, "Living with me, maybe three months. I met him about a month or two before that. So all together I've known him about five, six months."

"Okay," Gabriel said, looking at Jeff again. "Do you remember when the last time was with Hunter, in relation to that?"

"About two months, I think," Jeff whispered.

"Fine," Gabriel said, and he closed the chart. He looked up at Sean. "Based on that, I'd say that Jeff is safe. All that's left is to have you tested, Sean."

"I've been careful, Gabe," Sean growled.

"I have no doubt of that," Gabriel said, "but how long has it been since you last were with anyone before Jeff?"

"For fuck's sake, Gabe," Sean blustered, "there's a line between you as a friend and you as a doctor. Don't cross that line."

"Lighten up," Gabriel said with a hint of anger. "I'm not asking you for details. Based on test results and Jeff's knowledge of when he was last with Hunter, I know he's clean. According to your records, I haven't tested you in over a year. Since Jeff is clean, I want to make sure we keep him that way."

Sean growled again and squeezed Jeff's hand. "I haven't been with anyone since I met Jeff, but go ahead and stick me if it will make you happy."

Gabriel smiled in the face of Sean's anger. "You can have the blood test today."

Sean stood and pulled Jeff up with him. "Look, I appreciate everything you're doing for me and Jeff, Gabe—"

"Save it, Sean," Gabriel said as he stood. "I know these things aren't easy to talk about. Give me a minute to write up the lab slip."

While they waited, Sean pulled Jeff in close and whispered against the top of his head, "Everything is going to be okay, Tiger."

Jeff just nodded, feeling safe in Sean's embrace.

Soon Gabriel returned with the lab slip, and Jeff went to sit with him while the blood was drawn. Glad to see that Jeff had recovered some of his equilibrium, Gabriel turned to walk back down to his office. Appointments were done for the day, and he was anxious to type up his notes from the appointment. As he approached Mark's office, he slowed his steps.

"Again?"

Mark sounded angry. Gabriel knew it was wrong to eavesdrop, and as he stepped into the open doorway, he saw that Mark was turned away from the door, hunched over his phone.

"Well that's fucking great, Todd," Mark said. "I don't ask you for much, and you can't even do the small things I do ask you for." There was a pause, and then Mark continued, "Yeah, your job, well, fuck your job. Next time you say no I'll—"

Mark sat back and flipped the phone shut. When he turned and found Gabriel standing inside his office door, he snapped, "The fuck do you want? My life isn't your personal soap opera, Gabe."

Gabriel held up his hands. "Easy, Mark. I heard you halfway down the hall. Anything I can do to help?"

Mark's face was flushed, his hand clenched into a fist on his desk. He was silent for a long moment, and then he said, "No. Thanks."

"I'm here, if you need me," Gabriel said.

"Yeah, but for how long?" Mark murmured. "How long before you leave me in the dust when something better comes along?"

"Ouch," Gabriel said softly.

Mark reached up and ran a hand through his hair. "I'm sorry, Gabe, and I didn't mean that the way it sounded."

Realizing that Mark was still upset from the phone conversation, Gabriel turned to step out of his office again. He turned and said over his shoulder, "I'm done leaving you, Mark." He paused for a moment, then said, "I was done leaving you the day you came back."

"MMM," Sean said that night as they sat at the table in the kitchen. "I think this is the most delicious meal I've ever eaten."

"Really?" Jeff asked. He had made roasted salmon and potatoes and a salad of wild field greens with shaved Parmesan and was serving it with rolls from the bakery.

"Yes really," Sean said with a grin. "Where'd you learn to cook like that?"

Jeff shrugged. "TV. I watch a lot of cooking shows, and I just remember what they do."

"You're a natural," Sean said. "You could be a professional chef."

"Ah, you're just saying that," Jeff said.

"No, Jeff, I'm not," Sean said. "I never say things just to say them, you know that."

Blushing, Jeff picked up the plates and set them in the sink.

"So, do you feel more comfortable with Gabe now?" Sean asked as he leaned back in his chair.

"Yeah," Jeff said. "You were right; he's a nice guy, and he even wants to be friends with me. Do you want me to tell you what we talked about?"

Sean shook his head. "You don't have to, that's between you and him. He's my oldest and best friend, so it makes me happy that you like and trust him."

Jeff returned to sink into his chair again, and he said softly, "You are my best friend, Sean."

Sean stood, pulled Jeff up into his arms, nuzzled against his neck, and whispered, "And you are my sweet Tiger."

Chapter 11

Trust and Control

LIFE settled into a routine. Jeff fixed Sean's breakfast and sent him off to work each morning with a kiss. Within a week of Gabriel drawing Sean's blood, he called to report that Sean was also HIV negative.

After going over the information about the tutors, Jeff and Sean had settled on a center that wasn't far from Peachtree Clinic. This made everything easier for Jeff, since he already had that bus route memorized. Although it wasn't inexpensive for Jeff to visit the tutor every day, Sean had insisted that money was no object where Jeff was concerned.

At least once a week, Jeff stopped by to see if Gabriel was busy. Sometimes he just managed a quick hi, but other times Gabriel had time to sit and talk. Through these impromptu visits, a friendship did indeed flourish between them.

One afternoon they sat on a bench behind the clinic, and Gabriel pointed out where he lived, in a house behind the parking lot, joking that he never had traffic on his daily commute.

"So," Gabriel said as he loosened his tie, "how are things going?"

Jeff sighed and laced his fingers together. "I still can't read."

Gabriel suppressed his smile. "You've only been going to the tutor for a few weeks, Jeff. It takes time." He reached over and laid a hand on Jeff's wrist. "Don't get discouraged. Just keep it up, focus on the things that make you happy, and a hard task seems easier."

"Sean makes me happy," Jeff said softly.

"You make him happy too," Gabriel said. "Tell me about him."

"You know more about him than I do," Jeff said.

Gabriel shook his head. "We know him differently, that's all." He smiled and sat back against the bench. "What does Sean do that makes you happy?"

Warm color suffused Jeff's cheeks.

Gabriel chuckled. "Not like that, Jeff. Tell me what it is that Sean does that lets you grow and gain strength. How does he treat you differently from the way"—he paused for a moment and then said, "How does Sean treat you that's different from the way Jesse treated you?"

Jeff bit his lower lip, and his hands slid down in his lap to grip together. "Jesse never let me do anything for myself. He made all my decisions for me."

"And Sean?"

"He trusts me," Jeff said softly. "He encourages me, and he tells me I can do anything I want to do. He doesn't set limits for me because he believes in me." As he talked about Sean, his nervousness melted away, and he released his grip on his hands. "Sean is amazing. He knows so many things. He's patient, and whenever he looks at me, I get all fluttery inside, like I'm burning and freezing at the same time. Sean makes me feel things I've never felt before. He makes me feel like I'm his equal. He tells me I have courage, and I believe him."

"You do have courage, Jeff," Gabriel said.

Jeff blinked, as if he had been brought back to earth from his reverie. He turned and met Gabriel's eyes. "Before I met Sean, I would have never believed you."

"But you do now," Gabriel said with a smile.

"Yeah, I do a little," Jeff said softly.

"If you don't mind my asking, what was it like living with Jesse?"

"He's my dad," Jeff said softly.

"Legal guardian," Gabriel said, "although in reality he's not your guardian anymore, since you're over eighteen."

Jeff shrugged. "It's like he's my dad, though."

"And because you think of him as 'Dad', you are hesitant to say anything negative about him?" Gabriel said.

"I don't think I want to say anything at all," Jeff said with a sigh.

"You don't have to," Gabriel said as he shrugged.

"Sean doesn't like Jesse," Jeff said softly, at last.

"Does that bother you?" Gabriel asked.

Shaking his head, Jeff said, "I think what bothers me more is that Jesse doesn't like Sean."

"Why is that?" Gabriel said.

"Because," Jeff said, "I want Jesse to trust my decisions the way Sean does."

After a moment, Gabriel said, "Not trying to tell you what to do, Jeff, but eventually you're going to come to a place in your life where it won't really matter what Jesse thinks anymore. The more you live with Sean, the more your life will be wrapped up with his, and Jesse will fade to a memory."

A hummingbird flitted between the flowers growing along the edge of the parking lot, and at last Jeff said, "I guess you're right."

Soon after, he made his way home, and to fill the time waiting for Sean, he sat in the living room folding towels until eventually he drifted off to sleep. The pleasant dream that had been dogging him for weeks returned, and Sean found him sleeping soundly with a small smile on his lips.

"Jeff?" he said, waiting until Jeff opened his eyes. Then he continued, "Too tired to do your work?"

Jeff gasped and sat up. "I'm sorry," he mumbled, and he began to collect the clothes together, dumping them back into the basket. "I'll finish these in the other room. You don't want your living room looking like a laundry room." He hoisted the basket up on his hip and started into the bedroom.

Sean laughed. "I thought I was a neat freak, but you're even worse."

"I'm not," Jeff said over his shoulder, "but I know you are, and I shouldn't even have had the laundry in here, but I thought I'd be done before you came home. I was just so tired."

Sean followed Jeff into the bedroom. "It's your house, too, Tiger," he said. "If you want to fold laundry in the living room, it's okay."

Jeff stood nervously, plucking at the folded towels in the basket, and Sean came to stand closer.

"What's wrong? Did you think I'd be mad at you?" Sean asked as he laid his hand gently on Jeff's arm.

"No," Jeff whispered.

"Well, what is it, then?"

"I had a dream," Jeff whispered at last.

"Another bad dream?" Sean asked, and he turned Jeff so that they were facing one another.

"No," Jeff said, and he bit his lip as he looked up. "I think there's something wrong with me, Sean."

A slight frown creased Sean's brow, and he said, "Tell me the dream."

Color washed across Jeff's cheeks, and he pulled away and went to sit on the edge of the bed with his head bowed and his shoulders hunched forward. He said, "I dreamed I was pregnant."

Sean stood silently, watching Jeff.

At last Jeff looked up. "I thought you were going to laugh at me."

"Tell me more of the dream," Sean said after a quick shake of his head. Slowly he came closer and sat beside Jeff on the bed.

"I was in our bed," Jeff said hesitantly, "and my belly was all big, and you were kissing it and telling me how beautiful I was. And then you moved lower, and you sucked me into your mouth." His voice dropped lower. "It felt so good. And then, you went lower and...." He gasped. "I don't have the words to tell you."

"Jeff," Sean said, his voice low and urgent, "do you want to feel that?"

The color still flushed across his cheeks, Jeff said, "Yes, please."

Sean began to pull at Jeff's clothes until he lay back upon the bed, exposed to Sean's hungry eyes. He set the basket down on the floor and moved up to prop himself over Jeff, his hand down cupping Jeff's flat belly. "I wish," he said softly, "that my child could grow in your belly."

Jeff gasped, and Sean began to slide lower, kissing and nipping until he settled between Jeff's legs. His large hands covered the scars on both hips, and he opened his mouth to take Jeff firmly inside. A strong tongue circled Jeff's length and teased into the slit at the tip.

"Oh, Sean," Jeff said as he writhed against the bed. "Feels so good."

Sliding down to the base and then back up to the tip, Sean slid lower and touched the tip of his tongue to Jeff's balls. Jeff bowed up off the bed with another wail. Goosebumps covered his flesh as Sean gently took Jeff's balls into his mouth.

"Sean, please," Jeff murmured fitfully.

Releasing him, Sean whispered, "This is all for you, Tiger." He rose up and snatched one of the pillows from the head of the bed, lifted Jeff's hips, and tucked the pillow underneath. As Jeff settled, Sean continued licking at his balls and massaging his cock lightly with his hand.

When he went lower and touched Jeff's puckered entrance with the tip of his tongue, Jeff sucked his breath in and his cock jumped in Sean's hand. Sean tongued him gently, then prodded with his tongue and pushed inside, tightening his grip on the base of Jeff's cock to prevent him from spilling too soon.

Breath drawn in and eyes squeezed tightly shut, Jeff's body was as taut as a bowstring. When Sean whispered against the most intimate part of his body that he tasted good, it was enough to send him over the edge. With a prolonged wail, he came hard.

When Jeff opened his eyes he found Sean lying with his head along his side, quietly licking him clean. He reached down and laid his hand on the back of Sean's head. Sean eased up and kissed Jeff deeply. He gripped Jeff's wrist tightly when he felt him try to slip his hand under the waistband of his pants.

"Sleep now," Sean said.

"But you—"

Sean eased up on an elbow, his hand resting lightly on Jeff's belly. "Your dream was like a gift, Jeff," he said softly. "I've wanted my own child forever, but I know I'll never have one. Sometimes dreams feel real enough that they give us the things we really want." He bent down and kissed Jeff lightly. "Thank you."

"You'd be a great daddy, Sean," Jeff said.

"Maybe," Sean said, and he eased down beside Jeff again. "Sleep now. Dream of our little Liam again."

"Liam," Jeff said drowsily. "I like that name."

"Shh," Sean said.

Once Jeff had drifted to sleep, Sean stood and undressed, then slid in beside him and held him close. It was the truth that he wanted a child, but he had never been close enough to anyone to tell him that, let alone share the name he had selected. He nuzzled against the top of Jeff's head and marveled at how much he loved him.

WHEN Sean woke later, pulled from his dreams by a tickling sensation on his face, he found his eyes were covered. He struggled upward, hands flailing, and said, "Jeff?"

Jeff caught Sean's hands in both of his and held him still. "Shh, Sean," he whispered.

Sean lay still for a moment, taking a few deep breaths. He knew something was tied over his eyes, but aside from Jeff holding his hands, he was not otherwise restrained. Through the sleep haze in his brain, he realized that Jeff had covered his eyes for some reason. He just wasn't sure why. He strove to keep his voice level as he asked, "What are you doing?"

Jeff was silent at first, and then he bent down, his lips hovering over Sean's, and whispered against his mouth, "I want to taste you."

The tension began to ease from Sean's body. He arched up to claim a kiss and then settled back down against the bed. It was alien to him, allowing another to have control over his body, but he acknowledged as he eased back down against the pillow that being gentle with Jeff was an equally alien feeling. Something had snapped into focus for him that day in the park when he had taken the toy soldier from Jeff.

The tips of Jeff's hair tickled down Sean's body as he released his hands and began to move lower. He pressed his nose against the center of Sean's body and breathed in deeply of his unique scent until he pressed his lips against the head of Sean's cock.

Keeping his hands above his head as though they were bound, Sean spread his legs and moaned low in his throat. When Jeff settled between his legs and pressed his hips down to the bed, Sean moaned louder. Because he trusted Jeff, he could allow this control.

Jeff opened his mouth and slid halfway down Sean's length. He pulled up slowly and circled his tongue around the sensitive ridge at the tip, sliding his hand over to steady the base of Sean's cock.

"Mmm, Tiger," Sean rasped, and he bucked up slightly, pushing against Jeff's mouth.

The sound of Sean's voice encouraged Jeff, and on the next pass he sank all the way down to the base. Lightly grazing with his teeth on the upward pass, Jeff set up a slow and steady rhythm.

Sean groaned again and dug his feet into the mattress, using all of his willpower to stay still, afraid that if he bucked up against Jeff the heavenly blowjob would end. As it continued, he felt himself spinning out of control and desperately gripped his hands together above his head.

Jeff pulled up again, sliding his hand up to follow his mouth. He teased his pointed tongue into the slit at the head of Sean's cock and tightened his grip slightly.

Unable to hold still, Sean arched up and groaned. A light sheen of sweat covered his body, and every muscle was tensed. As though he could sense the emotions, Jeff reached up and took one of Sean's hands, threaded their fingers together, and waited until Sean subsided back against the bed before running his tongue down the pulsing vein on the underside of his cock. He ran his tongue over Sean's balls and drew the flesh into his mouth.

"Fuck," Sean growled, "feels so good."

Jeff moaned around Sean's flesh and then rose up to take his cock into his mouth again.

"Can't last," Sean murmured. "Can't last much longer."

One hand still tangled with Sean's, Jeff used his other to fondle Sean's balls and began bobbing his head faster. He felt Sean's release tremble through his balls first and then felt him explode into his mouth. His own moans matched Sean's, and he swallowed all he could before he eased off and laid his head on Sean's hip.

Too spent to reach for the blindfold, Sean unclenched his hand and lowered it down to cup the back of Jeff's head. His body sang with the release, and he struggled to catch his breath.

Jeff eased up the bed and pulled the blindfold away. His hair tangled across his eyes, and after making eye contact, he lowered himself down and kissed Sean, then pulled back enough to murmur, "You taste good."

Sean gathered Jeff close into a fierce hug, too overcome at the simple words to respond.

Chapter 12

A Handful of Dust

SEVEN months went by and spring gave way to summer and then autumn. On a gloriously blustery late fall day, Jeff and Sean were at Lullwater playing basketball. In the beginning Jeff hadn't enjoyed the game, complained it was too hard, but Sean had coaxed him, and now they raced up and down the court, breaking into a sweat.

"Two points!" Sean yelled as Jeff sank the last basket to tie up their game.

Jeff smiled and jogged back down the court. Sean held up his hand for a high five, and Jeff smacked it hard.

"Ow, Tiger," Sean said in mock pain. "I don't think you know your own strength!" He made a big show out of shaking his hand.

Jeff laughed and grabbed Sean's hand. "Then let me kiss it and make it all better."

With a mock roar, Sean pulled Jeff close against him and kissed him, oblivious to the fact that there were a few amused onlookers walking on the path nearby. Casually he released Jeff, and they went to flop on the grass where they had left their things. Sean dug two water bottles out of his bag and tossed one to Jeff.

Jeff broke the seal on the bottle and sipped at it, then wiped his face on the edge of his T-shirt. Sean had stripped off his shirt and poured half the bottle over his head. He chuckled as he watched Jeff, then reached over and grabbed the hem of his shirt.

"C'mon, Jeff, take it off and pour water over your head. You'll feel better!"

"Not here, Sean. People will look at me," Jeff said as he dipped his head.

"So what if they do?" Sean winked and said, "They might be staring at you with envy."

Jeff squirmed, but Sean was insistent. Once he pulled the shirt up over his head, Sean doused him with half a bottle of water.

"That's not so bad, is it?" Sean asked as he reclined back on the grass. He was the picture of power, strong muscled calves and arms with shorts that hugged the curve of his ass and the bulge of his cock.

"It's cold!" Jeff yelped.

"But it feels good, doesn't it?" Sean asked.

Jeff nodded and sipped some more of the water. He rolled on to his stomach, propped up on his elbows so he could watch Sean as he tipped his head back toward the sun. He realized that he always thought of himself in negative terms, and his self-image was low. He knew that if anyone felt envy when they looked at him, they'd envy the fact that he had landed such an attractive mate. As much as Sean tried to build him up, he realized he always knocked himself back down again. He rolled toward Sean and laid his cheek against his arm.

"Phew," he said. "You need a bath."

Sean laughed and said, "That's the smell of honest hard work, Tiger. But let's go home, and I'll shower so I don't offend your delicate nostrils."

"Hey, I know," Jeff said as they stood and collected their things. "Let me give you a bath."

"A bath?"

Jeff wasn't able to judge Sean's reaction, so he said nervously, "It's just that I got some new bath oil, it's called Sandalwood, and it's all masculine and stuff, and if you wanted, I could just run the bath for you, or you could just take a shower—"

Sean pressed his finger against Jeff's lips and winked. Jeff shivered and reached for his shirt, but Sean stopped him. "Let me look at you," he said in a soft, husky voice.

As they walked home, Jeff realized that Sean was indeed looking at him, and that he hadn't said he wanted to just to make Jeff feel good.

At home, they dropped their bags inside the door and Sean said, "Tell me where you want me, Tiger."

"Go get naked, Sean," Jeff said, his face coloring slightly, "and I'll tell you when I'm ready."

Sean grinned and headed into the bedroom to undress. He threw his clothes into the hamper, listening to the rustling sounds in the bathroom and the squeak of the pipes as the tub began to fill. At last he heard Jeff call his name, and he walked down the short hall into the bathroom.

Jeff had filled the deep tub and lit a few candles. When Sean breathed in deeply, he was satisfied with the musky scent of the bath oil.

"Mmm," he murmured as he stepped into the room and closed the door behind him. "Smells good."

"See?" Jeff said. "It's kind of masculine, isn't it?"

Noticing that Jeff still seemed a little nervous, Sean nodded and said, "Who knew I was involved with such a cultured guy? All the gourmet meals, and now this?" He stepped into the tub and sank into the fragrant water with a long sigh of pleasure.

"I never knew I could do all these things, Sean," Jeff said as he settled beside the tub. "I've never had anyone to pamper before." He picked up a cloth and dipped it into the water.

The water settled around Sean's neck, and he realized it had been a long time since he had had anyone pamper him or, more precisely, since he had allowed anyone to pamper him. "I think there are a lot of things buried inside you, Jeff," he murmured, "and I'm glad I'm here to discover them every day."

Jeff smiled and wrung the cloth out. "Every day there's something new. Like hanging a bag of dried lavender in the closet to keep your clothes smelling nice. Or putting a vanilla bean in a jar of sugar to make vanilla sugar for your coffee. Or using fabric softener so the sheets are soft for your skin."

"Or," Sean said, "seeing a tutor so you can get better at reading." He tipped his head to the side. "I don't need you here just so you can do nice things for me, Jeff. It makes me happy when you do things to help yourself too."

Jeff leaned forward and laid the cloth on Sean's chest. "You're good for me, Sean," he whispered, and then he scrubbed the cloth over Sean's skin. "Feel good?"

"Oh so good," Sean murmured. He watched through narrowed eyes as Jeff soaped the cloth and then raised it up to his face to breathe in the scent. When he lowered the cloth, a puff of the foam remained on his nose, and Sean reached up to brush it away.

"Sit forward so I can do your back," Jeff said softly.

"Your wish is my command," Sean said, and he bent forward, his cheek resting on his knees. He noticed that Jeff ran his hand along after the cloth, feeling his skin, and he realized that if it were anyone other than Jeff, he would never allow this.

"I love touching you," Jeff murmured.

Sean leaned back against the tub again and said, "I think there are parts of me you're missing," he said, and he winked.

Jeff's eyes widened. "There are?"

Sean laid his arms along the edge of the tub, spread his knees, and leaned his head back against the tiles. He nodded and watched as Jeff's eyes trailed over his body and understanding dawned.

Settling closer, Jeff laid a hand on Sean's knee and then dragged it down his leg and brushed against his cock. He bent forward and nibbled at Sean's ear as he closed his hand around Sean's burgeoning length.

"Mmm," Sean murmured as he turned and caught Jeff's lips. "Feels good."

As he returned the kiss, Jeff reached for the bottle of oil and poured some into his palm. He reached below the surface of the water and began to stroke again. "You feel so good, Sean, so alive," Jeff murmured.

Sean reached up and tangled his fingers through Jeff's hair. "You make me feel this way, Tiger," he growled. "I want you now, want to be inside you."

"But this was for you," Jeff said.

"It's what I want," Sean said. "Nothing better than finding pleasure together." He stood, and water sluiced off his body, some of it spilling on the floor.

Jeff handed him a fluffy towel, and after he blew out the candles, he followed Sean back down the hall to the bedroom.

Once they stood next to the bed, Sean pulled at Jeff's clothing roughly until Jeff stood pressed against Sean's warm, moist skin. Sean reached down to cup Jeff's ass and murmured, "I want you on your knees, Jeff."

Jeff tensed and buried his face against Sean's chest, assailed by memories of Hunter that he still strove to forget.

Knowing that something was bothering Jeff, Sean reached down and eased his chin up. "What's wrong?" he asked.

"I want...." Jeff paused, then took a deep breath. "I need to see your face, Sean, when you take me."

Sean rubbed his thumb over Jeff's cheek, then bent down to kiss him. "I can move the big mirror up by the foot of the bed, and then we can both see."

Jeff shivered. "You'd get me the moon if I asked for it, wouldn't you?"

Stepping back and releasing him, Sean turned to drag the mirror over by the foot of the bed. "The moon, and the moons of Saturn, Jupiter, and Mars... good enough?"

Jeff bit his lip, then whispered, "I love you, Sean."

Sean winked and came back to help Jeff climb onto the bed. He waited until Jeff settled on his knees, cheek against the soft coverlet, face turned to watch in the mirror. He trailed kisses down the curve of Jeff's spine.

Hands gripping the edge of the bed, Jeff shivered once as Sean's hips settled against him. He shivered again as Sean's lips caressed the smooth skin of his back. At last, with his cock resting snugly between the crack of Jeff's ass and his lips pressed against his neck, Sean murmured, "I'll never let you go, Jeff, and I promise you that I won't hurt you. Not ever."

"I know, Sean," Jeff whispered.

Sean straightened then, turning their bodies so that Jeff could watch as he ran his hands over his ass. He bent down and nosed along the crack of his ass, extended his tongue to massage Jeff's tight opening.

Jeff groaned, and as intent as he was on watching Sean, he let his eyes roam over the rest of his own body. From this distance he couldn't see the scars, and he tried to see himself through Sean's eyes.

Sparing a look into the mirror, Sean saw what Jeff was looking at, and he smiled. "That's it, Tiger, look at yourself, watch what's happening to you." He ran his hand up Jeff's back in a gentle caress.

With a small groan, Jeff arched up, his hair fringing over his back and Sean's fingers. He watched Sean lean back for the lube and wailed when he inserted a lubed finger into his passage. "It's good, Sean."

"Do you see?" Sean asked as he rocked his finger in deeper. "See how beautiful you are?"

Jeff tightened his grip on the covers, and what he saw in the mirror was how beautiful Sean was. He watched the expression on his face as he caressed Jeff's hip with one hand and fingered his ass with the other. He saw the care, the love that radiated from Sean's face, and in that moment, it superimposed itself over the ugly image in his head of Hunter taking him this way to humiliate him.

"Yes," he breathed then. "I see it."

Sean turned to meet Jeff's eyes in the mirror, and then he slowly slid his finger free. He picked up the condom packet and tore it open with his teeth. Keeping his eyes locked on Jeff, he slid the condom over his length, and then as he murmured, "Love you," he lined up and slid in with a firm thrust. "You feel like heaven around me, Tiger. Love being inside you."

Jeff pushed back against each forward thrust and shuddered with need as Sean reached under him to cup his erection up against his belly. "Oh," Jeff said, and he bit his lower lip between his teeth. Each thrust sent him closer to the edge.

"Come with me, Tiger," Sean urged.

So close to the edge, Jeff wailed with his release and was able to keep his eyes open long enough to see that moment of utter joy on Sean's face as he broke. He moaned as Sean bent down, still thrusting inside of him, and pressed his lips against his back.

When the climax passed, Sean slid free and pulled Jeff into his arms. They lay against one another, panting, until at last Jeff murmured, "Know what?"

"Mmm?" Sean murmured drowsily.

"I used to think that this," he gestured toward their intimately joined bodies, "was what I wanted all the time, and that I only felt strong when our bodies were joined. But I see now that this is what gives me strength for other times, when we're out in the world. I know there's a balance, and...." His voice trailed off.

"And?" Sean said.

"And you're right. I am beautiful because you make me beautiful," Jeff whispered.

"Mmm, Tiger," Sean said, turning to kiss Jeff's brow. "You're beautiful all on your own." He peeled off the condom and laid it aside.

Jeff snuggled closer, and they drifted to sleep.

THEY woke early the next morning, and after they each took a trip to the bathroom, they settled together under the warm covers.

"Sleep okay?" Sean asked lazily.

"Yeah," Jeff murmured. Then he said, "Sean, if I tell you something do you promise you won't get mad at me?"

Sean tensed slightly, and he said, "You know that usually when people say that, it's because whatever they're planning say is going to make the other person angry."

Jeff hesitated. "I'm not trying to make you angry, Sean, but last night when you took me on my knees like that, I was a little scared."

"Oh, Tiger," Sean said. "You should have told me. I don't want our lovemaking to scare you."

Jeff eased back. "Maybe that was the wrong word, then. You don't scare me Sean, but sometimes my memories do."

Sean tucked Jeff's hand in his. "You've had to live through some pretty scary stuff, Jeff."

"I think it's scarier now thinking about it than it was when I was living through it," Jeff said. He turned his back to Sean and settled down to spoon against him.

Sean settled his arm around Jeff's midsection. "Sometimes when you're going through something, you find strength that you don't know you have. Then, later, when it's all over, you feel fear."

"Guess I never thought about it that way," Jeff said softly.

"You're learning new things about yourself every day," Sean said.

They were silent for a bit, sharing their warmth, and then Jeff spoke again. "Hunter always did it that way, with me on my knees. It was like I was just a deposit box or something, like I wasn't even worth looking at. It hurt, Sean, not just a physical hurt, but"—he dragged Sean's hand up and laid it over his heart—"it hurt right here."

"Jeff," Sean said, pressing his hand tightly against his chest.

"Last night, I saw it doesn't have to be that way. I mean, I know you love me, Sean. I know that right here," Jeff said, tapping his finger over Sean's hand where it rested on his chest. "And it didn't hurt, and it didn't feel like you were trying to prove anything." He paused. "I can't make the words come out right."

"I think I understand, though," Sean said. "To me, it doesn't matter what position we're in, because, when I'm inside you, it's the most wonderful feeling in the world."

"I used to think that I didn't deserve you."

"But you don't think that any more, do you?" Sean asked.

Jeff twisted around to face Sean. "No." Tears welled in his eyes, and his voice cracked when he continued, "Last night, watching us...."

"You liked that," Sean whispered as he reached up to thumb away the only tear that fell.

"I did like it," Jeff murmured.

"Good," Sean said. "That's what I like to hear."

Jeff bit his lip. "Did you ever make a bad decision, Sean? Something that you thought was the right thing to do, and then you found out it was all wrong?"

"All the time, Jeff," Sean said. "It's a part of living."

"Yeah, I know," Jeff said, "but I mean a really important decision that affected your whole life. What if all of a sudden I started doing evil things to you?"

"I don't know what I'd do," Sean said, knowing what Jeff was driving at.

Jeff fidgeted with the edge of the sheet before he went on. "It's never going to happen, Sean, but it's just that I made some pretty fucked up decisions."

Sean put his hands over Jeff's, stilling them. "But you're different now, Jeff. You're clean and levelheaded."

"I used to think I was stupid for staying with Hunter, but now I think I was just too trusting. He wasn't honest with me."

As much as he wished he understood the dynamic that had sent Jeff headlong into the arms of a man like Hunter, Sean never asked. He wound his fingers tightly with Jeff's and said, "I'm honest enough to tell you that I can't promise I'll never lie to you, Jeff. I'm only human. But whenever you want to tell me something, just tell me. I'd rather have honesty between us than fear and pain."

"Okay," Jeff said, and his smile lit his face. "Last night you were snoring."

Sean gasped. "I don't snore!"

Jeff smiled. "Yes, you do."

"Knucklehead," Sean said, and he rolled over on top of Jeff, pinning him against the mattress. "You're going to have to make my breakfast now."

Jeff blushed and smiled. "I was going to do it anyway."

"Yeah," Sean said, "but now I want waffles and bacon, not just a slice of toast."

Jeff eased up and kissed the tip of Sean's nose. "Coming right up."

Chapter 13

Sins of the Father

BEING the oldest son of a single mother had taught Sean a lot about maturity. It had always seemed there was noise in the house, and there were times when his mother had joked that the only time she had any peace and quiet was when she locked herself in the bathroom. Once Sean had gone away to college, he had shed the family ties for good. He still loved his mom and his two brothers, but he believed in the notion that absence made the heart grow fonder.

Sean's middle brother had settled down and gone into business for himself shortly after he had graduated from high school. He was married with a passel of his own children, and without saying as much, it was clear he didn't approve of Sean's lifestyle. His younger brother Shannon had always idolized him; that much, Sean knew. Several years earlier, Shannon had flown the nest and come up from the family homestead in South Carolina to settle in Atlanta. Sean held him at arm's length but suffered semi-monthly visits. He had yet to introduce Jeff to Shannon, but he figured that would be the next logical step.

Instead of setting up the meeting, Sean found himself embroiled in one of Shannon's never-ending escapades. After calling him to re-establish contact, they had met, and the outcome was that he sat in the darkened living room, waiting for Jeff to come home. It wasn't often that Jeff went out on his own after dark, but Dakotah was out of dog food, and so he'd gone, promising to be careful.

The envelope lay on the table before Sean, shining like a beacon. He ran his hand through his hair nervously and sat up with a start when he heard Jeff in the kitchen, his singsong voice calming Dakotah, food pinging into the dog dish.

"Where are you, Sean?" Jeff called.

"In here," Sean said.

"Man," Jeff said as he came in and flopped down on the couch. He reached up and flipped on the lamp. "The store was so crowded, I didn't think I'd ever get through the line. Then I almost missed the bus." He cocked his head to the side. "Did you miss me?"

Sean smiled and said, "I always miss you when you go away." He held out his arm in invitation for Jeff to come and join him in the chair.

Jeff walked across the room gracefully and settled in Sean's lap. He kissed the tip of his nose and said, "What do you want for dinner? I was going to make spaghetti, but now it's too late, so I was thinking of warming up the leftover pizza."

"I'm not hungry," Sean said, and he pulled Jeff in close.

Jeff pulled back. "You feel okay?" he asked as he laid his hand on Sean's brow. "You're always hungry!"

Sean hesitated and bit his lip, and then he finally said, "I love you, Jeff."

"I love you too," Jeff said, and he settled back down against Sean's chest.

"Do you remember," Sean said slowly, "when I told you about my brother Shannon?"

"I think so," Jeff said. "He's the guy who's doing that martial arts thing, right?"

"Mmm-hmm," Sean said. "He's really serious about it. He moved into a training camp, actually, and trains at least twelve hours a day, sometimes more. He's very intense."

"Sounds like someone I know," Jeff said softly.

Sean smiled in spite of his nervousness, and then he said, "He ran into a little trouble with his girlfriend. She finally laid down an ultimatum, either the training or her, and he chose the training."

"Oh, Sean," Jeff said, and he turned to meet Sean's gaze. "I'd never do that to you. I promise."

"It's not that," Sean said. "You're more important to me than any business deal, any computer game. I'd never put you in a position where you felt the need to issue ultimatums." He paused, and then he said softly, "Turns out she's pregnant." He bent forward and picked up the envelope, opened it, and pulled out the ultrasound picture. "It's a perfectly formed little boy."

Jeff gasped and then reached out to lay his hand over Sean's as he held the picture. "Liam."

"Oh, Tiger," Sean said, and he bent forward to press his lips against Jeff's brow. "He wanted her to have an abortion, and she refused. She's going to put him up for adoption instead."

"He's your blood, Sean. You can't let him go to strangers," Jeff said, his voice fierce-sounding. "Don't make him go through what I went through with Jesse. Don't let him go to people who don't really want him."

Sean turned to lay the picture back on the table, and then he took Jeff's hand in his. "It's a big step, Jeff, not something anyone should enter into lightly."

"Ever since I had that dream where I was pregnant, I've been thinking about it, Sean, wishing there was some way I could give you a child. If I had a kid, then I could make up for everything I went through after my parents died, everything I went through with Jesse and the way he treated me." He paused to catch his breath. "Maybe your brother's child is as close as we'll ever get, and if you want to, I'd be proud to call him ours."

Sean swallowed hard and pulled Jeff back down into his arms. "You make me so happy, Jeff."

"Because you make me happy, Sean," Jeff said softly.

"I don't," Sean said, and then he stopped. He pressed his lips against the top of Jeff's head. "I don't want you to do this just to make me happy. It's a big responsibility."

Jeff was quiet for a moment, and then he said, "I'd do anything to make you happy, Sean, after all you've done for me. You've given me a home and encouragement and support. I know this is a big step, but I wouldn't do it just for you. I'd do it for Liam, so that he can have a happy life like he deserves." He turned to look up at Sean. "Besides, it would make me happy too."

Sean bent down and pressed his lips against Jeff's. "I'll check into it, then. There are probably a million hoops to jump through." He frowned slightly and said, "I have an old friend from college who is a lawyer. I haven't talked to him in years, but I'll call him, see if he can tell us what needs to be done."

Jeff snuggled in against him, and for the moment, they forgot about dinner.

IN THE end, they slept on it, and both were still committed the next morning. Adopting the unwanted baby was something they both wanted to do. Sean's ex from college, Andy, had gone on to become a lawyer, and Sean said he'd give him a call to see what all the ins and outs would be.

Even though he knew that it would be months and months before Liam joined their household, and because he refused to acknowledge that maybe he wouldn't, Jeff spent a happy afternoon shopping for the baby. When he came home late in the day, he found Sean in the living room reading the newspaper.

Jeff smiled and dumped all his bags on the coffee table. "You should see all the things I got for Liam today," he said happily.

The frown on Sean's brow disappeared, and he sat forward with a smile. "You're shopping for him already?"

"Yeah," Jeff said. He still wasn't able to wink, so he closed both his eyes. "I even got a surprise for you for later."

Sean chuckled. "Let's see what you got."

Jeff showed off the treasure trove of tiny T-shirts, receiving blankets, and a little stuffed panda bear. "The lady at the store said that when babies are little, they only see black and white. Think he'll like it?"

"I think he will, Tiger," Sean said. "Looks like Liam is going to be one spoiled little boy."

"Yeah, he's going to be spoiled," Jeff said. He sat back and said softly, "I got one more thing."

"What's that?" Sean asked, sensing Jeff's seriousness.

Jeff picked up the final bag and reverently pulled out a book. It had cute little bunnies on the cover, and Jeff traced the letters of the title with his fingers. He looked up at Sean and said, "This one says 'love'."

Sean held out his arms, and Jeff brought the book with him and settled in his lap. Nuzzling against his cheek, Sean said, "That word does say 'love,' Jeff. You're going to read this book to our little boy."

"We're going to read it together, you and me, Sean," Jeff said.

They sat in silence for a moment, and then Sean said, "I did some research today."

Jeff tensed slightly and sat back to watch Sean's face.

"It's not legal for you and me to adopt in Georgia because we're a same-sex couple. It's not legal for us to get married here for the same reason." Sean reached for Jeff's hand and twined their fingers together. "I can apply for guardianship, and because Shannon's my brother, they'll probably allow it. But just to cover all our bases, we should register as domestic partners."

"So, it's like," Jeff said, "like we're married?"

"Oh, Tiger," Sean said, pulling Jeff into the curve of his body. "This isn't the way I wanted to ask you. I wanted to have candlelight and get down on one knee." He paused when emotion clogged his voice. "I love you, Jeff, and regardless of laws and bullshit, I would view you as my husband."

Jeff made a choked sound, but before he could answer, there was a knock at the door.

"You expecting someone?" Sean murmured. Gently he eased Jeff out of his lap and then stood.

"Who would be coming to see me?" Jeff said.

"Don't know," Sean said, shrugging, "but whoever it is has a fucked sense of timing."

Sean opened the door, and from where he stood, Jeff couldn't see who it was. He just saw Sean's shoulders tense and heard the growled, "What the hell do you want?" The person outside the door gave some response, and Sean turned, the angry look on his face quickly replaced by controlled indifference.

"It's Jesse," he said tightly. "He says he wants to see you."

Jeff deflated and mumbled, "I guess you better let him in, then."

Sean stepped back and let Jesse walk into the room. Jesse approached Jeff and stood before him, hat in hand.

"Hey, Jeff," Jesse said. "How are you?"

Emotion still ran high through Jeff, a combination of the talk that had been interrupted between him and Sean and the unexpected arrival of the man he still thought of as his father. "I'm okay," he said at last. "What do you want?"

"Just wanted to see how you are, ask you when you're planning to come home." Whatever emotions Jesse was feeling, he kept them tightly in check.

"Home?" Jeff said with a snort. "I am home. This is my home."

"Since when do you consider this your home?" Jesse asked.

With a puzzled frown, Jeff said, "Since I started living here. You said it was okay."

"I didn't think you meant to move over here full-time," Jesse said.

"Well," Jeff said, "you said when I got better you wanted me to come work in your shop. You said that I could stay with you if I worked with you. I don't want to work in the shop. I told you that, so I kind of thought you would expect me to move out anyway." Slowly, he eased himself down to sit on the couch.

The movement brought Jesse's attention to the stacks of T-shirts and blankets on the table, and he frowned. "What's all this for?" He bent forward and plucked at one of the shirts.

Reverting back to his old ways, Jeff clasped his hands together and said, "Sean and I are going to adopt his brother's baby."

Jesse frowned and turned to look at Sean. "You put him up to this?"

Sean had remained standing just inside the door. His own hands clenched into fists. "You know what they say about assuming, don't you?"

In a flash, Jesse turned and closed the distance between him and Sean. "I know what they say, and I guess it makes assholes out of both of us." He tipped his head to the side. "I suppose you forced him into some kind of commitment behind my back?"

Unable to sit still any longer, Jeff flew out of his seat and tried to insert himself between the two men. "Nobody forced anybody to do anything, Jesse."

Jesse shifted his eyes from Sean to Jeff and said, "Then you want to explain this shit to me? This looks like one hell of a commitment to me, Jeff."

The anger that flashed through Jeff was evident in his eyes and the flush on his face. "I understand commitment, Jesse. I know a lot more about it than you do. I committed myself to Hunter for three years. I told him I'd stay with him, and I did, even when he started to break his promises to me. I let him do things to me that would make your hair curl because I believed in that commitment." He narrowed his eyes. "I stayed with him because I didn't think you would live up to your promises, and I didn't think you wanted me back, and I had no place to go." Jeff reached blindly for Sean's hand. "If you think I tied myself to Sean, it's because he lives up to his promises, and as hard as it is for you to believe, Sean loves me." Jeff's voice caught on a suppressed sob. "For the first time in my whole life, someone loves me for real."

Jesse reeled back and said, "For fuck's sake, Jeff, you have any idea what it was like having you and Luke thrust on me right on the heels of my old lady leaving me and taking my own kids away from me? Boil it right down, no, I didn't love either one of you, but I took you in and tried to do right by you. Hell, you never let me in close enough for me to know that prick Hunter was mistreating you. But give me a little credit. I came over here today to make sure you're doing okay and that you aren't being mistreated this time."

Sean stepped forward, shielding Jeff behind his larger frame. "I told you I wasn't going to hurt him."

Ignoring Sean, Jesse continued, "You say this is the first time anyone's loved you for real, but what about Luke? What about your brother, you think he never loved you?"

Jeff dipped his head. "It's not the same."

"You chased him away, Jeff," Jesse said. "He went away to school and never came back."

Hot color flushed over Jeff's cheeks. "Maybe it was my fault that Luke went away, but I've changed a lot, Jesse," he said. "I've grown a lot, and I've realized a lot. You never wanted me, and the only reason you're here now is because you feel guilty."

Jesse made a sound of irritation and shoved his hands into his pockets. "Maybe that's the case, but I ain't taking nothing for granted anymore."

A whirl of emotions crossed over Jeff's face, and he swallowed hard. He moved closer to Sean and then said in a soft voice, "I'm happy here, Jesse. I want this child with Sean, and I want this life with him. You came over here. You see that it's not like it was with Hunter. Now just go away and leave me alone." He stepped back away from Sean, and his voice broke as he said, "I don't want you here anymore." With that, he turned and walked from the room.

Sean watched Jeff until he disappeared into the bedroom, and then he turned on Jesse. "Listen, asshole, I haven't liked you from the moment I laid eyes on you."

Jesse's lip curled with contempt. "I guess the feeling is mutual, then. I just hope Jeff's willing to lie in the bed he made himself."

"Bed he made himself? What the fuck are you talking about?" Sean flexed the muscles in his arms.

"This bed. Here. With you," Jesse said.

"Being here with me was a choice Jeff made for himself. Adopting my brother's child is a decision we made together. As hard as it is for you to understand this, Jeff is very capable of making his own decisions. If you can't be happy with that, it's your own goddamned fault."

Jesse's eyes widened. "My fault? How you figure Jeff getting himself in the middle of this situation is my fault? How are you gonna feel when the kid starts waking you up in the middle of the night or pukes all over your nice things? I hope you thought all that out before you got him all excited about having a baby. I don't see how any of that is my fault."

Sean advanced, backing Jesse against the door, all the vitriol he'd felt for this man from that first day in the park tumbling out. "I'm aware of the ups and downs of having a child. Jeff and I have discussed all the angles. I'm sure there will be surprises, but Jeff and I are willing and able to handle them all, together." He paused to take a breath and then continued in a deadly soft voice. "What I meant is that it's your own fault that Jeff doesn't want you to be a part of his life anymore, and he won't let you be a part of his child's life. The state may not recognize a marriage between us, but that doesn't mean there won't be a commitment ceremony."

"That's convenient," Jesse said with a smirk. "Talk of a commitment ceremony now. A little like shutting the barn door after the cows are out."

Sean laughed mirthlessly. "I don't have to listen to any more of this bullshit. You came, you saw, now get the fuck out of my house."

Jesse's face flushed, and he bent closer to say in a deceptively soft voice, "Don't fucking push me, boy."

Sean stepped back, raised his hands, and shoved Jesse backward. "I just did."

"Why don't we take this outside?" Jesse said. "Wouldn't want to disturb the runt."

"Fine," Sean said, reaching behind him to open the door. "You made him so miserable for so long. You have no idea how long I've wanted to just fuck you up."

They walked down the front stairs and out into the middle of the yard. Jesse turned and raised his fists. "Bring it, then."

"I've wanted to beat your ass to a pulp for all the times I've listened to Jeff telling me you treated him like a worthless piece of shit, for neglecting him when he was struggling in school." Sean shoved Jesse again, hard enough to make him lose his balance.

"There are two sides to every story, and you're just hearing the one side," Jesse said, and then he smiled. "You think beating up on me is going to change all that, then go ahead and try."

Sean lunged forward, knocked Jesse to the ground, and landed a hard right to his jaw. "It don't change nothing, but maybe it will beat into your head that you're just as much at fault as he is. You have a hell of a nerve letting all this time pass before coming over here and trying to get back in his life again. If you were this bothered about it, why did you let him start staying over here in the first place?"

Jesse surged up and rolled them over so he had Sean pinned to the ground and dug his knee into Sean's chest. "You're the one who's got a hell of a nerve, talking to me like that, boy. When I told him he could stay here, I didn't realize he meant to pull up stakes and move in with you."

Sean brought his knee up hard into Jesse's gut and reversed their positions. "What's wrong with him moving in here with me? I'm taking the responsibility with him that you never did. I took him to a doctor, got his dyslexia diagnosed, got him the help he needed to get on the right path. Way I see it, I've already done a lot more for him than you ever did."

Jesse brought up his knee, but Sean blocked it. "I can't change what's in the past," Jesse said with a grunt. "I can only admit that I didn't pay as much attention to him as I should have because I was sunk into my own problems. It just don't set right with me, you doing all this shit for him just so you can rope him into a commitment to house your brother's bastard."

Sean reached over and grabbed the front of Jesse's shirt and pulled him close. "You better think twice before you bring my family into this. You must have a pretty warped sense of reality if you think I'm doing things for Jeff because I want something out of him. Everything I've done for him is because I love him, and I want him to be happy."

Jesse reached over to grab Sean's shirt and pulled him so close that their foreheads were touching. "You better fucking mean that, Murphy, because if you ever"—he paused to give emphasis to his words—"ever do anything to hurt him like that piece of shit Hunter did, you'll regret it for the rest of your life."

Through gritted teeth, Sean said, "I will swear to any god you name that Jeff will never want for anything, material or spiritual, while he's with me."

"You better make sure that's a promise you mean to keep," Jesse said, releasing his grip, "because I sure as hell mean to keep the one I just made you."

Sean rose to his feet, watching as Jesse struggled upright too. "I don't make empty promises," he said. "Or empty threats."

Jesse straightened his shoulders. "I'll be watching you."

"Go ahead," Sean said, and he turned and walked back up into the house, slamming the door behind him.

Chapter 14

Moonbeams

IT WAS fully dark by the time Jesse left. Sean went back in the house and found Jeff had remained in the bedroom. He stood at the back window, arms folded over his chest, staring out at the yard. Sean pulled his shirt up over his head, bunched it up, and threw it toward the corner.

Jeff whirled, and with one look at Sean's sweaty chest, he knew what he had already suspected: they had fought. Uncrossing his arms, he came across the room and flung himself against Sean, wrapping his arms around his waist.

"Is he gone?" he asked.

"Yeah," Sean said, "he's gone."

"I'm sorry, Sean," Jeff whispered. "I don't know why he came over here."

"It's not your fault, Tiger," Sean said as he looped his arms around Jeff's waist. "Don't ever take the blame for something you didn't do."

Jeff moved his arms up around Sean's neck, pushed hard against him, and nibbled at his jaw.

"Whoa," Sean said. "What's gotten into you?" It was rare for Jeff to initiate contact between them.

"You, Sean," Jeff murmured. "I want you, need you."

Adrenaline still pumping, Sean reached up for Jeff's hands and pinned them behind his back. He bent down low over Jeff's face and said fiercely, "Then have me, Jeff."

"Have?" Jeff shivered.

Releasing Jeff's arms, Sean reached down for the hem of Jeff's shirt and yanked it up over his head. "You set the pace, Jeff," he growled, and he worked on freeing himself from shoes and jeans. "I want you just as much as you want me." He started to work on Jeff's pants and then pushed him back toward the bed.

"I'm not sure," Jeff said softly as he watched Sean lie back on the bed.

Sean was the picture of power, still sweaty from the fight, cock hard against his belly, one knee drawn up. He narrowed his eyes and said, "I am."

With a small wail, Jeff climbed up on the bed, settled between Sean's outspread legs, and then eased up for a kiss. Sean reached up to pull him down hard against him so that their cocks nestled together. He pulled back from the bruising kiss and said, "You know what to do. Whatever feels right."

Jeff pushed himself up, rearranging their bodies until he was straddling Sean. Moonlight streamed in through the window, illuminating them both in a silvery glow. Jeff skimmed his hands up Sean's chest, teasing over nipples that peaked immediately at the stimulation. Struck by sudden inspiration, he arched his head back and reached down to close a hand around his own erection.

"Until I met you, Sean," Jeff whispered as he tightened his grip and stroked up the length of his cock, "this only felt right when it was just me." He moaned low in his throat as he slipped his hand back down on his own length, falling into a natural rhythm as he stroked himself. "I always wondered how it would be, to have someone who loved me back touching me, and I pretended"—he tipped his head far enough that he could meet Sean's gaze—"like this."

Sean's cock twitched against his body as he watched Jeff's erotic show. Although it wasn't really what he'd had in mind when he asked Jeff to take the lead, he enjoyed it nonetheless.

Lost in the sensations he was causing, Jeff moaned and eased forward, his knuckles brushing over Sean's belly as he continued stroking himself. "Never felt this good," he murmured, "until I met you."

"You're amazing, Tiger," Sean crooned. He reached up and joined his hand to Jeff's, stroking along with him. "I want you so much."

Woken from the spell, Jeff rolled his head down, looking down at Sean through strands of his hair. He released his hand from his cock and let Sean take over, then swept his hands over Sean's chest, stopping to tweak at his nipple.

"That's it, Jeff," Sean said. "Whatever you want."

"I want you," Jeff's voice was barely above a whisper, "inside me, Sean."

"Not yet," Sean murmured. "Let me see you in the moonlight first."

Jeff arched back again, a fat drop of pre-cum dripping down across Sean's knuckles. "Want you very much, Sean, please."

With a growl he didn't bother to stifle, Sean let the adrenaline take over again. Twisting his hips, he pushed Jeff off his body, let him settle down against the bed. Knees on either side of Jeff's hips and hands on the bed beside his head, he bent down and kissed him.

Surging up, Jeff wound both arms around Sean's neck and gave in fully to the kiss.

When it broke naturally, Sean pulled up and opened the drawer on the bedside table, extracting lube and a condom. Although need sang through his body, he took the time to gently prepare Jeff. One finger, then two, twisting and stretching his passage.

Jeff plucked his fingers against Sean's shoulders, spreading his legs wider. He groped for the condom, tore the package open, and before Sean slid his fingers free, Jeff was already sliding the condom into place on Sean's shaft.

"I like it, Jeff," Sean growled softly, "when you're eager this way."

"Always eager," Jeff mewled. "Just really need you tonight."

"Wait," Sean said as he rose up on his knees. He squirted an extra line of lube on the outside of the condom. "Don't want to hurt you," he said, panting. "Can't hold back."

Jeff clutched at Sean's neck, stifling a howl that could have been either pain or pleasure as Sean pushed inside. He pulled up, burying his face against Sean's neck.

"You okay?" Sean said with effort.

Instead of answering, Jeff nodded, let go, and fell back against the bed. Holding back long enough to judge that the expression that covered Jeff's face was not fraught with pain, Sean gave way and began to pump inside him.

Jeff erupted first, arms spread wide on the bed, the howl of pleasure caught in his throat as the intensity of the release washed through him. Unable to hold back, Sean followed closely, his roar making up for Jeff's silence.

When the tremors passed, Sean rolled down to face Jeff, found his hand, and held it up against his chest, pressing his lips against the knuckles. "If anything good came out of Jesse coming over here," he murmured, "then it was this."

Jeff bent closer, and a shiver ran down his spine. "I wish he didn't come over here right when you were in the middle of asking me… what you were asking me."

"Wishes don't change the past, Jeff," Sean said. "Only we can stamp out the ugliness. If there was a way to do that, then you coming out of your shell was it." He slid his hand down and cupped Jeff's ass. "There won't be a wedding, just a ceremony of promise. But Jesse won't be here for it."

Jeff was quiet for a bit, digesting what Sean said, and then he finally said, "You mean that I should forget he came here and ruined my happiness because we made our own happiness instead."

"Something like that," Sean said. He reached down and peeled the condom off, setting it behind him in a dish on the bedside table. "But if you wanted, we could invite your brother."

Jeff buried his face against Sean's neck, his voice muffled. "He won't come. I chased him away just like Jesse said."

"But he's your brother," Sean murmured, "and even though I know that brothers can be a pain in the ass, I know that there's a deeper bond than we realize between us sometimes."

Jeff was quiet for a moment, digesting that. "I tormented Luke, and after he graduated from high school, he went to college. Didn't come back here until he had graduated and had a job teaching at the junior college. I don't think he wants anything to do with me. I said some bad things to him."

Sean eased his hand away from Jeff's ass and moved to trace over the Hs on his hip. "We can try to get a hold of him, see if he wants to come over for a visit," he said. "Let you two get reacquainted. You don't know, Jeff, until you try."

"Maybe," Jeff said.

"Only if you want," Sean said. "I'll never push you to do things you don't want to do."

"But you just did," Jeff said.

"Not really," Sean said. He trailed his hand down and gently stroked Jeff's cock. "Being the one in charge is something you've wanted, but you chicken out."

Jeff was quiet for a bit, and then he moaned as Sean tightened his grip. "You always make me see reason, Sean."

Stilling his hand, Sean moved closer and nuzzled at Jeff's lips, and then he pulled back and said, "I thought you said you got me a surprise today."

Jeff smiled. "I did." He eased back and took the discarded condom and package and dropped them into the wastebasket. "Wait right here."

Sean grinned and watched Jeff scamper from the room, glad to see that his good mood was restored. His was, too, he acknowledged, but the memory of the fight still rankled, and it would be a while before that disappeared. Soon Jeff bounded back through the door and climbed back up on the bed. He turned on the bedside lamp and put a small bag in Sean's lap.

"What's this?" Sean asked, and he eased up against the headboard.

"Your surprise," Jeff said.

Sean upended the bag, and a pile of black and purple silk slithered out. He plucked at the pile and found two pairs of boxers. "Wow," he said. "I've never had silk shorts before."

Jeff pulled the purple pair away and said, "These are mine, and those are yours." He bent forward and whispered, "I think black makes you look sexy."

Sean chuckled and pulled Jeff down against him again. "Shut out that light, Tiger. I want to see you by moonlight again."

With a shiver, Jeff turned off the light and settled on his back. Sean propped up on an elbow and gazed down at him. "I love you," he whispered.

Jeff turned his head and gazed up at Sean. He mouthed, "Love you."

Chapter 15

Thicker Than Water

THE week after Jesse came to visit, Jeff stopped by to see Gabriel. In the beginning, Jeff had been shy about intruding on Gabriel at work, but over time, they had in fact become friends, just as Gabriel had predicted. Usually Jeff stopped by at the end of the workday, but this time he had so many things on his mind that he had come at lunchtime. Gabriel was just finishing with a patient, so Jeff sat in his office to wait.

As he waited for Gabriel to join him, Jeff sat with his knees pulled up on his chair, chin propped in his hand as he watched the fish swim around in Gabriel's desktop aquarium.

"I think I should just give you the aquarium, Jeff," Gabriel said as he entered the room.

"Oh," Jeff said, startled. "The fish would miss you, Gabriel, and I couldn't take them." He fell silent, watching Gabriel settle at his desk. "You ever wonder if they'd like it in a bigger aquarium?"

Gabriel blinked and turned to face Jeff with a mildly bemused look on his face. "You're a conundrum, Jeff," he said.

"I don't know what that means," Jeff said.

Gabriel cocked his head to the side. "You're a riddle."

Jeff resettled in the chair. "Is that a good thing or a bad thing?"

"It's a Jeff thing," Gabriel said with a laugh.

With a wan smile, Jeff opened the bag that contained the sandwiches he had made and said, "I know you like chicken, so I made chicken salad."

"Wow," Gabriel said as he took the thick sandwich. "I didn't know you could cook."

"Anyone can make a sandwich," Jeff said, and he paused as he remembered an early conversation he had had with Sean. Instead of picking up his sandwich, he clasped his hands together in his lap.

"Looks like you have a lot of things on your mind today," Gabriel said as he reached for a napkin.

"How do you know?" Jeff asked.

"For starters, I haven't seen you do that with your hands in a long time. I thought you were getting more comfortable with me," Gabriel said.

"I am comfortable," Jeff said, and he forced his hands apart.

"Well, then what's going on?" Gabriel asked, his expression mild.

"Too many things," Jeff said.

"It's always a good idea to start at the beginning," Gabriel said.

"You sound just like Sean when you say that," Jeff murmured.

Gabriel grinned. "Great minds think alike, you know," he said, and he winked. "Speaking of, he says your reading lessons are going great and that you started to read him a book the other night."

"He told you that?" Jeff blushed, and as soon as he said the words, he put his hand over his mouth.

A slight frown creased Gabriel's brow, and he said, "Maybe you better tell me some of your 'too many things,' Jeff."

Jeff dipped his head and mumbled, "Jesse came over."

"Tell me about that," Gabriel said.

"He said he wanted me to come home with him, but I told him I was already home." Jeff continued to stare at the floor instead of turning to make eye contact with Gabriel.

Gabriel watched Jeff in silence, waiting for him to continue.

"I got really pissed, Gabriel, and I accused him of ignoring me when I really needed him, even though I know he had a lot of his own problems at the time. I told him he just felt guilty and that he never really wanted me. I guess I was pretty selfish." Jeff stopped, pulled his hair back from his face, twisted it up behind his head, and let it fall before he continued. "Then, when he found out we're going to adopt Liam, he said some pretty ugly things. I actually touched him in anger, and I had no right to do that, to be so disrespectful."

"Why do you think that?" Gabriel asked.

"Because he's my dad, legal guardian, whatever you call it. I owe him respect even though he never really gave me any respect." Jeff looked away, back to the fish tank. "But...."

"But what?" Gabriel prompted.

"Sean didn't agree when I told him that. He said I had every right to say what I did." Jeff's face flushed with color again.

Gabriel was quiet for a moment, and his voice was soft when he finally spoke. "Jeff, your feelings are your feelings. It's not up to me, it's not even up to Sean, to tell you how to feel about things. I just hope that one day you'll see that Jesse has no hold over you anymore. You're your own man, and you make your own decisions. You don't need his permission to be happy."

Slowly, Jeff eased his hands down in his lap again, clutching them together. He was silent for the longest time, and then he said, "That's what Sean said, too, but for some reason it makes more sense when you say it." He looked over at Gabriel. "Thanks."

"You don't have to thank me for telling you the truth," Gabriel said. "That's one thing. What are some of the other things you have on your mind?"

"When Jesse came over, he mentioned my brother Luke. He said it was my fault Luke went away," Jeff said.

"Luke," Gabriel said. "I've never heard you talk about him before. Why don't you tell me a little about him?"

Jeff fidgeted in his chair, and Gabriel waited for him to continue.

Jeff picked up his sandwich and took a bite as if stalling for time. At last he set it aside and took a long drink of water before he continued. "Luke's three years older than me. I think that after they made him, my parents thought he was perfection, and everything that came after was just dregs." Although there was a bitter tinge to Jeff's voice, his expression was blank. "Luke was my cushion against the world, against the criticism I got from my parents. He never believed I should try to be more like him, and he always told me I should be like me. I looked up to him for the longest time."

"What changed?" Gabriel said softly in the silence that followed.

"After Mom and Dad died, we went to live with Jesse. Luke was pretty devastated. I was, too, but since I didn't have the connection with them that he did, I think I was numb. Jesse's wife had just left him, took his own kids away. Instead of looking at us like replacements, he just thought we were a burden. I figured out that he hated me more than my parents did, and Luke wasn't my protection anymore." Jeff shrugged, and his eyes hardened around the edges as he went back into that remembered pain. "I started hanging around with the wrong kind of people."

Gabriel nodded. "The friends who convinced you to drop out of school."

"Yeah, and take drugs," Jeff said. After another silence, he continued. "Worst thing was, I started to take things out on Luke. I said really ugly things to him, stuff I can never take back. He never fought back; he just let me make him more miserable than he ever was. Even though I was wasted all the time, I could see the pain in his eyes just increase by the day. When he graduated from high school, he went away to college, and he never came back."

"You know," Gabriel said, "sometimes we're harder on the ones we love than we are on anyone else. Sometimes they understand it, and sometimes they don't." He turned to look at Jeff. "I think if you saw your brother now, things would be different. You think you can't take back the things you said, but time mellows things, and he might surprise you."

Jeff turned away, lost in thought. Finally he murmured, "I wonder."

"If you want, I can call Jesse, try to find out how to get in touch with Luke," Gabriel said.

"You'd do that for me?" Jeff asked, tears welling in his eyes. "Sean said he would, but I don't think he wants to talk to Jesse again."

Gabriel reached over and laid a hand on Jeff's arm. "If it would make you happy, I'll call him."

"It would," Jeff whispered.

As Gabriel pulled his hand back, he said, "Speaking of Sean, how are things with him?"

"Fine," Jeff said quickly.

Gabriel quirked his lips into a small smirk. "When people say 'fine' that quickly, they're trying to hide something. Earlier, you seemed surprised when I told you that Sean says your reading lessons are going well. Sean loves you, Jeff. Why do you think he wouldn't be supportive of you? Why does it surprise you that he says nice things about you behind your back?"

Jeff sighed and closed his eyes. "Things seem different," he finally murmured.

"How are they different? It might help to talk about it," Gabriel prodded. "That's what friends are for, after all, to help when things seem bad."

"I can't, Gabriel," Jeff said softly. "You and Sean are good friends, and I can't put you in the middle of anything between me and Sean."

"You and I are good friends, too, Jeff," Gabriel said. "You should know that whatever we talk about is between you and me."

Jeff hesitated and then said haltingly, "Sean's the first person who ever made me feel good about myself, who ever believed in me. But ever since Jesse came over, things seem different. Yesterday I accidentally broke one of his coffee mugs, and he yelled at me."

"He's human, Jeff. He has some very real faults," Gabriel said.

"I always thought he was perfect," Jeff said quietly.

"It's hard to have your illusions shattered," Gabriel said, "but no one is perfect. This is something you need to talk to him about, though, if it's bothering you."

Jeff slid his hands back down in his lap as he clasped them together. "I can't talk to him about something like that, Gabriel. I'm too much of a weakling."

"If you can't talk to him about things like this now, how are you going to deal with issues after Liam comes along?" Gabriel asked firmly.

Jeff covered his face with his hands. Gabriel looked on for a moment, then he turned his chair toward Jeff's. He reached over and turned Jeff's chair so that they were facing each other and laid his hands on Jeff's knees.

"I'm not trying to upset you, Jeff. Really, I'm not," Gabriel said. "It's just that if you're going to commit your life to him and a child, and if you love him, then you need to be able to talk to him. About anything."

"But," Jeff said, his voice muffled behind his hands, "you're so much easier to talk to, Gabriel. He scares me sometimes." Slowly he lowered his hands and met Gabriel's gaze.

"Why does he scare you?" Gabriel asked.

"Because he's so fierce. You're soft, and he's only soft sometimes." Color rushed to Jeff's face as he said the words.

Gabriel smiled. "Sometimes Sean and I are exact opposites, but that's what makes our friendship so strong. You and he are opposites in a lot of ways, and if you let it, that diversity will bond you tighter."

"Sometimes I wish things were easier."

Before he could respond, Gabriel's phone buzzed, and his receptionist reminded him that he had patients waiting. Both men stood, and Gabriel took Jeff's hand. "Things will get easier, Jeff, because you'll make them easier."

Although he looked uncertain, Jeff nodded and said, "Thanks for everything, Gabriel."

"You don't have to thank me," Gabriel said. Then, to lighten the mood, he said, "This was the best chicken salad I've ever had. What did you put in it?"

Shaking his shoulders to free himself of the melancholy, Jeff said, "Walnuts, dried cranberries, it was just a regular chicken salad."

Gabriel picked up the sandwich bags and threw them away. "Well, it was delicious. You're going to spoil me, because I'll want your regular chicken salad more often."

They walked from the office together, and Jeff had a lot more things on his mind.

Chapter 16

Out of the Past

SEAN had always liked the park, even before Jeff walked into his life there. There was something soothing about the sun on his shoulders and covert people-watching. It was on the Emory campus and served as the commons. During the second half of his college days, he and Andy had been inseparable, frequently meeting at the park between classes.

If he were honest with himself now, Sean would have to admit that there had been a discrepancy between him and Andy back in the days when they had spent lazy afternoons sprawled on the grass at the park or, more frequently, sprawled naked across Sean's bed. He had never wanted to acknowledge the longing for a stronger commitment he'd always seen in the depths of Andy's eyes. Sean had made himself believe that when they ended their relationship just after graduation it was what they both wanted. In the intervening years, when communication from Andy had ceased, Sean had finally admitted that he had inadvertently broken Andy's heart. If not for this sudden need to confer with a lawyer, Sean would have left well enough alone, but through the grapevine, he had discovered that Andy's position with one of the top law firms in downtown Atlanta was as a specialist in contract law. Swallowing his pride, Sean had given the firm a call, and Andy had agreed to meet and talk through the specifics of domestic partnership and adopting a child.

Now, as Sean sat waiting on a bench, firing French fries as missiles at a cluster of pigeons, he thought back to an afternoon in the distant past and the familiar feel of Andy's skin under his fingertips.

"So, what's on tap for the rest of the afternoon?" Sean asked as he popped the top off a beer bottle and settled down on the couch.

Taking his own bottle from the small fridge, Andy settled down beside Sean and answered in a low voice, "Well, I was hoping I could talk you into writing a paper for me."

Sean arched a brow as he turned and lifted a knee up on the couch beside him, faced Andy, and said, "Write a paper for you? You know, you'd have to pay for that."

With a shiver, Andy turned his head. "That's what I was hoping you'd say. No one's better at writing papers than you, Sean."

"Writing them? Or making you pay me for writing them?" Sean said huskily as he leaned closer.

With a stifled groan, Andy leaned forward and set his bottle on the table. "You're good at both, Sean." He slipped from his spot on the couch and moved over to kneel in front of Sean.

"What's the topic?" Sean asked as he shifted, spread his legs so that he framed Andy between them.

"Battle of the Bulge," Andy whispered. He trailed a hand up Sean's leg, rested it over the growing bulge in Sean's jeans.

Sean growled low in his throat and swept his shirt up over the top of his head, leaving his hair a wild mess. He bent closer and cupped Andy's face between two large hands and murmured, "If you want me to write this paper for you, and you're not just making it up so that I'll fuck you, tell me where the battle took place." He ran a thumb gently over Andy's cheek.

Taking a deep breath and nestling into Sean's caress, Andy murmured, "Belgium. Started in December 1944, crossed over into January 1945." He paused to lick his lips and then said, "They called it the bulge because it was the first time the Germans cut into the Allies' line of advance."

"Good boy," Sean crooned, and he drew his hand back and leaned back against the couch. "You can have your cake and eat it too."

With a rakish smile, Andy rose up on his knees and deftly unsnapped the front of Sean's jeans, easing them and the briefs down to reveal Sean's swollen cock. "I know better than to lie to you, Sean," he said as he bent forward and touched his lips to the head of Sean's cock. Flicking his tongue over the ruby head, he murmured, "If I lie to you, I don't get what I want."

"Damn straight," Sean murmured. He stretched both arms along the top edge of the couch and slid lower.

Steadying the base of Sean's cock with his hand, Andy began to slide his mouth down until his nose nudged against the bush of hair covering Sean's sack. Sean groaned his approval as he pushed up against him, feeling himself sliding even farther down Andy's throat.

"You do that so good, my little cocksucker," Sean said affectionately.

Andy growled and formed an even tighter suction, letting his hand follow his mouth. He rose up to the tip and flicked his tongue across Sean rapidly, causing him to moan even louder and tighten his hands into fists. Andy slipped his hand up and down Sean's length as he continued to tease his tongue down under the ridge.

"Take it, Andy," Sean said on a ragged moan. "Take it all the way again."

Rising up on his knees, Andy angled his head so that Sean slipped all the way down inside his throat again. One hand worked down the crack of his ass and pushed into him a little. Sean was reduced to wordless moaning. Andy bobbed faster, his hair tickling against Sean's belly. Finally, he raised up again and murmured around the tip of his cock, "Don't hold back anymore… come for me… I'll take it all."

Sean growled, and he thrust his hips up off the couch again as Andy's finger found his spot. Unable to hold back any longer, he filled Andy's mouth with his boiling release. He unclenched his fists and gripped Andy's shoulders tightly as he curled up toward him. Andy never lost the rhythm, swallowing and stroking until Sean collapsed back against the couch again. He released Sean with a soft pop and then gazed up the length of his body. Sean met his eyes for a moment, then reached down and hauled Andy up into his arms.

He closed his mouth over Andy's hungrily, kissing him deeply, sharing the last remains of his release. "Just because I'm doing you a favor," Sean said hoarsely when the kiss ended, "don't mean this all has to be one-sided."

"Wasn't thinking it was going to be," Andy whispered.

"Then you're wearing too many clothes," Sean said.

With a chuckle, Andy stood and shed his clothes while Sean tossed the cushions from the back of the couch to the floor. He settled back and catcalled as Andy dropped his shorts. "Better lock the door in case Gabe gets home early."

"Want I should just put a sock on the doorknob?" Andy said as he flipped the deadbolt.

"Cute," Sean said.

Stepping over the strewn clothing and cushions from the couch, Andy made his way back and tumbled down against Sean's body. "Where were we?" he murmured.

"Right here," Sean said as he grazed his hand down the front of Andy's body and closed it around his cock. He squeezed gently as he nibbled against the juncture of neck and shoulder.

With a loud, growling moan, Andy arched up against Sean's hand.

"Easy," Sean murmured. "We have a long night ahead of us."

"'M greedy, Sean, fuck," Andy moaned.

"I like you greedy," Sean said as he cupped Andy's balls and extended one long finger down between the halves of his ass. As he teased against his puckered hole, he murmured, "You ready to break our record?"

Not even bothering to try to suppress the shudder that chased down his spine, Andy gasped, "You mean tonight we go for eight?"

One hand clamped over Andy's belly to hold him close, Sean eased his finger inside and growled, "That's what I mean...."

"Trying to kill them?" Andy drawled slowly, bringing Sean back from the depths of the reverie.

Startled, Sean looked up, then stood and pulled his dark glasses off. "Andy," he said.

Extending his hand, Andy pulled Sean into a bear hug. "Been too fucking long, Sean," he said.

"I thought you wanted nothing to do with me," Sean murmured.

"And yet you still called when you needed help," Andy said as he stepped back. "Kind of like the old days, only the tables are turned, eh?"

Sean chuckled. "You planning to make me pay you for your help?"

Andy's eyes flared for the briefest moment, and then soft color flooded his cheeks, and he said softly, "No, Sean, no one's going to pay for this."

"Sorry," Sean said as he sank back down on the bench. "Poor choice of words."

"No worries," Andy said as he sat down beside Sean. "You and me, Sean, we were a long time ago. Things are different now. I wasted a lot of time being pissed at you." He shrugged. "Then a funny thing happened: I woke up one day and got on with my life." He reached over and laid a hand on Sean's knee. "Nothing's ever going to take away the things we shared."

With the memory still fresh in his mind, Sean took a deep breath and said, "True, that."

"So," Andy said as he pulled his hand back, "reckless Sean Murphy's taking responsibility these days. Steady relationship and taking on a child. The only vestige of the old you is this penchant for killing pigeons with French fries. I'd think you'd be the happiest man in Atlanta. What gives?"

Sean heaved a sigh and wadded up his fast food bag. "Would you believe I was just nervous about seeing you again after all this time?"

Andy snorted. "You? Nervous? Try again."

Sean smirked and tossed his bag toward the bin, just barely banking it in.

"You worried about the guardianship?" Andy asked. "You have two roads you can choose. Since the child is your brother's son, you can outright adopt, but that will be tricky, since you and Jeff haven't been filed as domestic partners for that long. Your other route is guardianship, but then again, it would be you named as the guardian. After your partnership with Jeff is in place a little longer, there's a chance he can be named as guardian, too, but that only happens in special circumstances."

"I didn't file the domestic partnership papers yet," Sean said softly.

"What's the holdup?" Andy asked.

"I'm not sure if it's any one thing," Sean muttered, "or a bunch of little things."

Andy leaned forward and laced his fingers together. "Well, maybe you better tell me what's on your mind, then, Sean. Let me know if I'm spinning my wheels for nothing."

"It's not for nothing," Sean said, a hint of anger in his voice. "Jeff wants this child more than anything, more than he even wants me, I think."

"So," Andy said slowly, "you're hesitant because you think that if you give him a child, he'll stop thinking about you two as a couple? It's a common problem, Sean. Trust me, I know. But it usually happens with people who aren't as committed to a relationship with each other or have hidden items on their respective agendas. I haven't met Jeff, but from what you say, he isn't that type."

"Fuck," Sean said. "Sometimes I just feel so restless, like I'm not a whole person anymore."

Andy frowned. "You're losing me, Sean. Going out on a limb here, and you can smack me if I'm wrong, but you don't feel like a whole person anymore because you've given part of yourself to Jeff?"

"Yes. No. Hell, I don't know," Sean said.

"There're things you're not telling me, Sean. Spill it," Andy said.

"I love Jeff," Sean murmured.

"That's a start," Andy said, "but something about making your partnership a legal one is making you nervous. That's normal."

"It's not just that," Sean said.

"What is it then?"

"Look, I know we just went over this, and what's in the past is in the past, but of everyone I ever hit the sack with, you were the one I respected the most. You kept up with me; you gave back as good as you got. I still remember breaking the record." Subconsciously mimicking Jeff, Sean clasped his hands together in his lap. "Sometimes I wonder if Jeff and I are right for each other."

"Whoa, Sean," Andy said, "we had something once, but—"

"I didn't mean I want to pick up with you again. We had something good, but it doesn't compare with what I have with Jeff. It's just...." Sean sighed.

"What?" Andy said.

"Jeff fills me with feelings I've never felt before, good things. He's allowed me to learn things about myself that I never knew, but I feel like something is missing. Something about what I was like before, the way it was with you and me. I can't cut loose like that with him. He doesn't match me in bed the way you did." Sean turned away, a muscle tensing in his jaw. "It's starting to bother me."

Andy sucked in his breath. "Look, Sean, when we were together, everything was raw sex. You're right. I wanted more, and you broke my heart when you dumped me. I just got done telling you that. But I also told you that I moved on. Hell, everyone we knew back in college has moved on except you. That's why when Gabe told me that you finally grew some maturity and settled down with this guy Jeff, I was glad. Change is good, and whether you know it or not, this core of sensitivity has always been there inside you."

Sean heaved a great sigh. "I need things he can't give me," he said.

"It ain't none of my business," Andy said, "but how do you know he can't give you what you think you need? You ever talked to him about it?"

"No. How the hell am I supposed to ask him if it's all right if I fuck his brains out seven times a night without caring if I hurt him or not?"

"All I'm saying," Andy said, standing, "is that if you have doubts, it's not fair to keep them from him. You need to talk things out, and the sooner the better, if you want this process of taking in your brother's baby to go smoothly." He put his sunglasses on. "As for the sex, you and I both know there's ways to ask without asking. He might surprise you."

Sean reached into his pocket and pulled out his shades. He put them on as he stood and reached for Andy's hand. "I hear you," he said, "and I'll be in touch."

Andy squeezed Sean's hand. "It was good seeing you, Sean. Let's don't be strangers."

"That's a promise," Sean said.

Chapter 17

Wicked Game

MANY nights, Gabriel burned the midnight oil. His house was directly behind the clinic, but it was just easier to work in his office, even though that often meant he was walking back home well after midnight.

On a night like this, when exhaustion threatened before he was done with his paperwork, he burned a small candle. The soft glow and pleasing scent kept him focused.

With all the boring paperwork done, Gabriel cleared the screen and searched his desktop icons until he found the folder labeled "Jeff." It was always a good way to end the day, thinking about Jeff and his progress. He wasn't sure why he was keeping notes about his talks with Jeff, but it had always been part of his nature as a doctor to chronicle things. These weren't official notes; he just kept them because he enjoyed seeing how Jeff was progressing.

Jeff asked me about the aquarium today. I offered to give it to him, but he said he thinks the fish would miss me. In the next breath, he wondered what would happen if the fish were released into a bigger aquarium. He doesn't realize that he is like that fish in my small aquarium, floating around in his little world of Sean. I'd love to release him into the big world, watch him blossom even more.

Gabriel looked up as he heard a noise down the hall, then smiled ruefully as he realized he wasn't the only one still in the clinic burning the midnight oil. Without wondering why Mark was still there, as he usually left shortly after five, Gabriel went back to typing in his notes about Jeff.

Jeff does seem to be making progress in the matter of thinking of himself as a whole person. I sense that his recent confrontation with his guardian was beneficial in that respect. He mentioned today that he is also keen to renew a relationship with his brother. I will endeavor to help him regain contact with his brother, as I believe that will help him grow further.

Gabriel hesitated, his fingers hovering over the keys before he continued typing.

He has also reported there has been a change in his relationship with Sean.

There was a louder noise; this one sounded like Mark had thrown something across the room. Abandoning his contemplation of Jeff, Gabriel pushed back from his desk, blew out the candle, and walked out into the hallway to investigate. Light spilled from Mark's office, and Gabriel could just make out a soft grunt as another loud thump came from the room. He quickened his pace in time to reach the door of Mark's office and found him slumping heavily into his chair.

"Mark?" Gabriel said.

"What the fuck are you doing here?" Mark asked, not bothering to look up at Gabriel.

"I work here?" Gabriel said. As he walked into the office, he noted that the wastebasket brimmed with items that had lately been on Mark's desk: a picture of Mark with his boyfriend Todd, a small box, and the pressed rose in a frame.

Sighing heavily, Mark leaned back in his chair. "Go home, Gabe," he muttered. "There's nothing you can do here."

Gabriel dragged a chair around the edge of the desk and plopped down in it, reaching out to put his hands on the arms of Mark's chair, effectively blocking him into it.

"What happened, Mark?" he asked.

"Todd left me," Mark said, emotion making his voice raw. He opened his eyes and looked directly into Gabriel's. "You know a little something about that, Gabriel, don't you? Leaving me, hurting me."

"Don't," Gabriel said, moving his hand over to grip Mark's wrist.

Mark crumbled and dipped his head. He was silent for a moment and then drew his breath in on a sob. "His job has always been more important to him than me. He got an offer to relocate out to California, and he took it. Thought I'd follow him like a puppy. They need doctors everywhere, he said." He looked up. "Took the job without even asking me, Gabe, didn't even make me part of his decision-making."

Gabriel tightened his hold on Mark's wrist. "That's rough, Mark. I'm so sorry."

Tears leaked from Mark's eyes, and he turned his head from Gabriel's intense expression. "It's not like I don't have any practice with it, though, is it, Gabe?"

"Look," Gabriel said, "I know it hurts, but I told you… I know what I did to you was wrong, Mark. I admitted that to you." He released his hold and pushed his chair back. "Take as long as you need to get past this, and when you're ready, I am too."

Mark turned back. "You better mean that, Gabriel Romano. I've already got a pretty fucked self-image, and this didn't help."

"I mean it," Gabriel said softly. He bent forward, and as he breathed in Mark's scent, he was assailed with memories. "You know where I'll be."

"I know," Mark said, "but I need some space."

Reluctantly, Gabriel stood and rounded the desk. "Space I can give you, Mark. I just don't want…."

"I hear you," Mark said.

As Gabriel made the short walk home, the memory that had been evoked by Mark's scent began to form in his head. He had been hurrying across campus in the dark, much like this very night....

The party was still in full swing, but all Gabriel could think about was the fact that Mark wasn't there and had said he would be. He replayed the events of the day in his head. In the morning, he had received final confirmation that he had been accepted to the med school program back home at Brown University. After the graduation ceremony, he had had a quick glimpse of Mark before he hurried off to work. During a graduation lunch, Gabriel had shared his plans with Andy and Sean. Then he and Sean had gone off to make the final payment on their graduation trip, and Andy had headed off to play pool. Then came the party and Andy's evasiveness every time Gabriel wondered where Mark was. Eventually, an inkling had formed in his head, and he'd left the party against the weak protests of Andy and Sean and headed straight for Mark.

When he arrived at Mark's apartment, he knocked on the door, but there was no answer. He rapped his knuckle against the door again and called out softly, "Mark?"

Still no answer, so he laid his ear against the door and heard music playing softly. "Why don't you answer the door?" he muttered, fishing for his key.

The interior of the apartment was dark. The music was coming from Mark's bedroom, and Gabriel winced when he recognized the song and Chris Isaak's plaintive voice.

"What a wicked game we play." The last line was punctuated by a sniffle, and that roused Gabriel from his hesitation. He strode swiftly into the room, and the sight that met him took his breath away.

The room was dark, and Mark sat on the bed, gazing out the window. He turned his head slightly when Gabriel entered the room, and the moonlight glinted off the tracks of his tears. Gabriel stood helplessly gazing at him as Mark flipped the tape off and turned to look out the window again. He drew his knees up against his chest and hugged them tightly.

"Go away," Mark whispered.

Gabriel approached him slowly and perched on the edge of the bed. "Why?"

With a snort, Mark wiped angrily at his eyes. "Why? Because I don't want you here, that's why."

"Baby," Gabriel said as he reached out and laid his hand on Mark's back.

"Leave me alone," Mark gasped, jerking away.

Gabriel looked at him in amazement. "What's wrong?"

Mark turned, anger creeping across his features. "What's wrong? You're either incredibly stupid, Gabriel Romano, or you're a cold, unfeeling bastard. Maybe it's a combination of both, and maybe it will make you a great doctor. But right now I want you to get the fuck out of my apartment. Go back to your graduation party."

"I came here looking for you because you said you'd come," Gabriel said.

"Changed my mind," Mark said, turning away toward the window again.

Gabriel stared at him in silence for a moment and then said softly, "Want to tell me what's going on here, Mark?"

With a snort, Mark said, "When were you going to tell me?"

"Tell you what?"

"That you're leaving," Mark whispered. "That you're going back home to Rhode Island."

Gabriel dipped his head. "Who told you?"

"What the fuck difference does it make who told me? I know now. I know that all the plans we made together, right here in this bed, tangled up in each other's arms,—" His voice cracked, and new tears spilled down his cheeks. "You lied to me, Gabriel."

"No," Gabriel said, looking at him. "It was not a lie. I was going to tell you. I just hadn't found the right time yet."

"Well when was that right time going to be? After you fucked me again?"

"That's not fair, Mark," Gabriel said.

Mark uncurled himself and stood. "Not fair? You really are an arrogant son of a bitch, aren't you?" He turned and strode angrily across the room. "All I know is that you're throwing all our plans away like yesterday's trash." His voice rose in agitation. "And you don't even have the balls to tell me yourself. I have to hear it from that prick Andy."

Gabriel stood and approached him. "Look, Mark." He sighed and ran a hand through his hair. "I didn't tell you myself because I was waiting for the right time. I just found out for sure this morning."

"This morning?" Mark swallowed heavily. "Do you think I'm a fucking moron, Gabe? You must have been planning this for quite some time. Applications to med school don't just manifest themselves in a morning."

Gabriel dipped his head guiltily. "I went to visit the campus when I was home at Christmas break. Submitted my application then." He tilted his head and looked up at Mark. "I didn't tell you because I didn't want to think about leaving you, baby."

Mark put his hands up over his face. "Stop it. Just go back to your party." He sank down on his knees. "Go, Gabe. Just get out of here."

"No, damn it," Gabriel said, sinking down to face Mark, an angry edge entering his voice. "We sort this out now." His grip tightened on Mark's wrist.

Mark's head dipped lower, and he moaned.

"Damn you, Mark," Gabriel said, yanking on his hand. "Answer me."

"No," Mark said, looking up. Two spots of bright color burned on his cheeks, faintly visible in the moonlight. "It's over. You and me. It's over, and you know it."

Gabriel loosened his grip and let Mark's hand fall free. "It's not over."

"Yes it is," Mark said, shoulders slumping. When he spoke again, his voice was barely above a whisper. "After you leave here, you'll forget all about me."

"No," Gabriel said. "I won't forget you, Mark. Can't forget you."

Mark looked up at him, tears leaking down his cheeks again. "Then... make it so I can't forget. Fuck me... give me something to remember you by."

Gabriel stared at Mark for a long moment, then pulled him into his arms almost brutally, a fierceness entering him. He'd always been gentle with Mark previously, carefully taking his time, but not now. He broke away from the kiss, panting, and reached down and tugged the loose shorts down Mark's body.

Mark moaned as he kicked the shorts free and knelt on his hands and knees on the floor in front of Gabriel. The sound of Gabriel's zipper grating open caused him to shiver. He gripped the edge of the rug when Gabriel fingered him roughly.

"Do it," Mark wailed. "Oh God, Gabe."

Gabriel hastily stroked lube on his erection, positioned, and drove in with one hard thrust, grunting with the effort. Mark whimpered against the floor and gripped the rug tighter. Gabriel backed out and slammed into him again, his hands crushing Mark's hips, their bodies slapping together.

Heedless of the fact that he was likely hurting Mark, Gabriel increased the pace. His hand crept up to grip Mark's shoulder tightly, and his breath hitched in the back of his throat. He reached under Mark and began to stroke him, squeezing him rhythmically.

At last, with a strangled cry, Mark came, his issue boiling through Gabriel's fist, pooling on the rug below him. His wild spasms brought about Gabriel's release, yet neither seemed to take pleasure. When Gabriel's body stilled, Mark rolled away into a tight little ball, crying softly. Gabriel sighed and lay on the floor behind him, wanting to touch him yet needing to give him his space.

Eventually, Mark quieted, and his breathing evened out with sleep. Gabriel retrieved a blanket from the bed and covered them both. He lay awake staring at the ceiling for a long time before he finally drifted into an uneasy sleep himself.

The memory had faded by the time Gabriel poured a glass of wine with a shaky hand. The next morning, they had talked out all the different angles but had come to the conclusion that there was no way to continue the relationship. Neither of them wanted to end things with bitterness on both sides. After the talk had died out, they had made love one more time, giving each other something to remember the other by.

As he sat in his darkened living room, sipping the wine slowly, Gabriel admitted to himself that he was perversely glad that Mark was single again. Although he had had a few casual relationships in the interim, there had never been anyone to match Mark. Seeing Sean happy had set the longing desire burning in Gabriel again. He would make every effort to play his cards right this time.

Chapter 18

Making Amends

THE smell of cinnamon and apples filled the kitchen as Jeff peeked in to check on his pie. A gentle rain fell outside, pattering against the windows. Dakotah was curled up in his bed; the twitching of his nose now and then was the only sign that he was awake.

Jeff sat at the kitchen table and pulled the crinkled brochure out of his pocket. Carefully, he smoothed it out on the table and gazed at it longingly again. The wedding rings all had Celtic designs, and Jeff had already chosen the one he would give to Sean if he had the money.

"What do you think, Kotah?" he said softly. "You think Sean would like this one, or maybe this one?"

The only indication that the dog heard was that his tail thumped against the floor.

"Gabriel says," Jeff went on, "that I have to tell Sean the things that are bothering me." He turned and looked down at Dakotah. "You think it's true what they say, that the way to a man's heart is through his stomach?"

Dakotah jumped up and came over to lay his nose on Jeff's knee. "I know the way to your heart is through your stomach, Kotah," Jeff murmured. He ruffled the dog's ears, then got up and got him a treat from the jar on the counter.

The timer buzzed, and Jeff took the pie out of the oven and set it on the cooling rack. Alone in the house, he wandered into the living room. Sean wouldn't be home for a couple of hours, and all his chores were caught up. Jeff flopped down on the couch and picked up his sketchbook. It had been a while since he had drawn anything, and he idly flipped through the pages until he found the pictures he had made of Sean. The pictures still stirred him as much as the memory of dreaming about Sean back in the days after they had first met.

Before he drifted too deeply into his reverie, there was a knock at the door. Frowning, he stood, fearing that Jesse had come back now that Sean was gone at work. He tiptoed to the door and looked out through the peephole and found his brother Luke standing on the porch. He gasped and wrenched the door open just as Luke turned to walk away.

"Luke?"

Luke turned back, shoved his hands in his pockets. "Hey, Jeff."

Jeff flung himself against Luke, knocking him off balance.

"It's okay, munchkin," Luke said softly. "I got you." He pulled his hands from his pockets and wrapped his arms around his brother.

"Didn't think you'd want anything to do with me," Jeff said as the tears started. "I'm so sorry, Luke."

"Hey, now," Luke crooned, and he freed a hand to stroke Jeff's hair. "You're still my brother. What's in the past is in the past."

They stood silently for several moments, sharing that bond that brothers have, the one that had been damaged but never broken. At last Jeff stood back, took Luke's hand, and pulled him inside the house. "Did Gabriel call you?" he asked.

"Dr. Romano? Yeah, he said he thought it would mean a lot to you if I came by." Once inside, Luke gazed curiously around the neat living room. "Jesse called too," he said softly. "Said you were having a rough time of things." A small frown creased his brow.

Jeff made a sound of irritation. "Jesse don't know shit about shit," he said, and he resumed his seat on the couch. He closed his sketchbook and clasped it against his chest. "My rough times are done. I'm happy now with Sean."

"That the guy Jesse told me about?" Luke asked as he took a seat beside Jeff on the couch. "Jesse thinks Sean is taking advantage of you."

"Jesse just doesn't get it. Hunter took advantage of me. Sean's the best thing that's ever happened to me in my whole life." His voice dropped to a whisper. "He's the only person who has ever really loved me for me."

A pained expression crossed Luke's features. "That ain't true, Jeff. I've always loved you for who you are. You refused to believe it, is all."

Quick tears welled in Jeff's eyes, and he clutched his sketchbook tighter. "I... I'm sorry, Luke."

"No more 'sorrys', munchkin," Luke said. He reached over and laid a hand on Jeff's knee. "Jesse says this guy Sean is making you do things you shouldn't, like he has you wrapped around his finger or something. He says he's talked you into taking in his brother's illegitimate child."

Jeff flung the sketchbook aside and stood in agitation. "I'm not wrapped around Sean's finger. I don't know why nobody thinks I can make my own decisions." He whirled, his eyes blazing with fury. "Did you just come here to take Jesse's side? Because if you did, you might as well leave right now."

"Easy, munchkin," Luke said as he stood and wrapped his arms around Jeff. "I'm not here to judge you, and I'm not here to drive the wedge further between us. I lost you once, and I'm not going to lose you again." He laid his cheek against Jeff's soft hair.

Deflating at the soft words, Jeff raised his arms and wrapped them around Luke's waist. "Don't judge Sean until you meet him, Luke," he said raggedly. "We want Liam. I want him because I don't want him to suffer all the hurt I did when our mom and dad died."

Luke caressed Jeff's back gently. "You must be pretty serious if you've already got a name picked out for him."

Jeff stepped back, went to sit on the couch again. "We had the name before we even knew we were going to have him."

Joining him on the couch, Luke tipped his head to the side and said, "I don't want to set you off again, but I'm just curious. Do you know for sure that you're going to get him? Don't they, I mean...." His voice trailed off.

"Sean has a friend that's a lawyer. He said Sean can adopt Liam because he's Liam's uncle, but I would have to wait for some kind of special.... I don't remember what he said. It's just that...."

"What?" Luke asked softly.

"We have to be registered domestic partners for everything to go smoothly, and we're not yet." Jeff picked up a sofa cushion and hugged it tightly.

"Why not?" Luke asked.

Jeff shrugged. "I don't know. We just haven't done it yet."

The silence that fell between them was broken by the sound of Sean's SUV pulling into the driveway and then Dakotah's nails on the kitchen floor as he ran to greet him. Both Jeff and Luke stood.

"Mmm, Tiger," Sean called from the kitchen, "did you make this for me?" When he entered the living room, he stopped short, a look of puzzlement on his face.

Jeff walked over and eased up for a kiss. Then he said, "Sean, this is my brother Luke. Gabriel called him and told him I wanted to see him again."

A smile broke out on Sean's face, and he extended his hand. "Luke, so nice to meet you."

Luke took his hand and smiled too. "Nice to meet you too." He released Sean's hand and said, "Jeff's been telling me about Liam."

Sean's smile faltered only slightly, and then he put his arm around Jeff's shoulders. "He likes to brag," he said evenly.

"Why don't I fix us some pie?" Jeff said, and he slipped away to head for the kitchen.

"Let me help you," Luke said.

Sean followed them into the kitchen and sat at the table as Luke and Jeff served the pie. "So," he said as he slid his napkin into his lap, "I know you're Jeff's brother, but that's about it."

Luke smiled as he took his seat and picked up his fork. "I teach English literature over at Atlanta Metro," he said. "Been there about a year."

"You a full professor?" Sean asked as he sectioned off a bite of pie.

"Don't give him the fifth degree, Sean," Jeff said as he took his seat.

"It's okay, munchkin, I don't mind," Luke said. "Associate professor, working toward full professorship. My goal is to eventually transfer to Georgia State. Got a few more years ahead of me before that comes about."

Sean grunted as he took another bite of pie. "Sounds like you've got your career path all set out," he said.

"Pretty much," Luke said.

Conversation was kept to neutral topics as they finished their pie. Luke gathered the plates and set them in the sink, then said he needed to be going. Jeff urged Luke to come again soon, and Sean told him he was welcome any time. After Luke left, Jeff came back to sit at the table with Sean. Gabriel's words welled up in his memory again.

"Was the pie good?" he asked softly.

"Anything you make is always good, Tiger," Sean said.

Jeff chewed his lip, looked up to meet Sean's eyes, and then said, "I went to the mall today."

Sean sighed. "Jeff, don't keep spending money on the child. We don't even have him yet."

Jeff cringed and said, "I didn't." He pulled the crumpled brochure from his pocket and smoothed it out on the table. "I was looking at these."

Sean sat forward, and when he saw it was wedding bands, he let his breath out in a long sigh. They sat in silence for a few minutes before Sean pushed his chair back from the table and walked out of the kitchen.

Jeff stared after him in shocked silence, and when he heard the sound of Sean's computer games, he bent his head forward. It had been a long time since Sean had closeted himself in his office to play the games. Before long, a tear tracked down Jeff's cheek, and he stood and tossed the brochure into the trash bin.

Chapter 19

The Best-Laid Plans

SEAN glanced up from the computer screen and saw that the windows were no longer dark. He reached up to rub his bleary eyes and pushed back from the computer desk. It had been months since he'd spent the entire night playing games. In fact, he hadn't done it once since Jeff had come to stay. His circle of online friends had embraced him wholeheartedly and chided him gently for neglecting them.

With a sigh, Sean shut down his computer and stood up from the chair. He paced restlessly around the edge of his desk and stood lost in thought next to the battle scene. A full quarter of the table was given up to the medieval battle scene he and Jeff had started together and never finished. Idly, he picked up one of the models and turned it over in his hand, allowing his mind to drift.

He wasn't proud of stalking out of the kitchen the day before when Jeff had showed him the rings, and Andy's stern words had been cold comfort as the long night wore on. He wasn't sure what bothered him more, Jeff's innocence or the fact that he was shirking his supposed duty. When had things gotten this complicated?

As he set the knight back into the battle scene, the answer occurred to him. His life had gone from simple to complicated the day he had run after Dakotah in the park, and he wasn't sure if that was a good thing or a bad thing.

When the phone rang, he jumped, and as he turned to retrieve it, he saw that the sky had gone from gray to the pearly light of dawn.

"Hello?" He cradled the phone against his shoulder.

"Hey Sean, it's Shan."

"Hey, Shan, what's up?" Instinctively, Sean realized this couldn't be a social call if Shannon was calling so early.

"Look, Sean, I have some news, and it's bad news. I don't want to beat around the bush, so I'm just gonna come right out and say it."

"That's always the best plan," Sean said as he pulled his chair out from the desk and sat. "Shoot."

"About the adoption," Shannon said. "It looks like it's not going to happen."

"What?" Sean said, sitting up straight.

"I'm sorry, Sean, it's just that—" Shannon hesitated.

"It's just that what, Shan? This is going to kill Jeff. You better give me a good reason." Sean clenched his hand into a fist on the desk.

"She decided to keep it," Shannon said, an apologetic tone in his voice. "I agreed to pay her child support, and, well… there's a chance we'll get back together."

"Fuck," Sean said. He unclenched his fist and raised his hand to cover his face. "You've got balls of steel to bring this up now after everything I've been through over this."

"You've been through? Jesus Christ, Sean, it's just like you to make things all about you," Shannon said. "Some things never change."

"Do you have any idea how much this child means to Jeff?" Sean said.

"I don't know, Sean, but I bet it ain't half as much as it means to Cindy," Shannon said acidly. "Look, I'm sorry your boyfriend got all worked up over this, but that's the way it's going to be. We're keeping the child."

"'Sorry' ain't gonna cut it," Sean said.

"You're an arrogant prick, Sean Murphy," Shannon said.

"I love you, too, bro," Sean retorted.

"Call me back when you simmer down," Shannon said, "but I ain't gonna change my mind."

Sean pulled the phone away from his ear when the line went dead, and he tossed it aside. Both hands up to rub his face now, he leaned back in his chair, cursing softly.

Before long, Sean heard Jeff moving about in the kitchen. He sighed and got up to go out and join him.

Jeff bit his lip when Sean walked into the kitchen. He cleared his throat and said, "Did you sleep?"

Sean opened his arms, and Jeff walked into them. Sean wrapped his arms tightly around Jeff and mumbled, "No, I didn't." He bent down to press his lips against Jeff's cheek and whispered, "I'm sorry I ran out on you yesterday, Tiger."

Jeff stiffened slightly and said, "No, Sean, you don't gotta apologize. It wasn't my place to look at rings without you."

"It's your place to do whatever you want, Jeff. It's not my place to make you feel bad for the things you do." Sean tucked his knuckle under Jeff's chin and raised it up. He waited until Jeff focused, then said softly, "We need to talk, Tiger."

"I know," Jeff said, and he shivered in Sean's embrace.

"Shannon called this morning," Sean said. "There's no easy way for me to say this, but he had some bad news."

A frown creased Jeff's brow, and he tucked his cheek down next to Sean's chest. "What is it?"

"I don't know how to say it so it won't hurt you, Jeff, but he and his girlfriend have decided they want to try to work things out. They're keeping the baby, so Liam won't be ours after all."

"What?" Jeff said, pushing back from Sean. "What do you mean? I don't—I thought—" In agitation, he pushed away completely. "I thought they didn't want him. How can they change their minds like that? I don't understand."

"Shh," Sean said, reaching for Jeff again, pulling him back into his arms. "Shannon agreed to pay her child support, and they're going to work on patching things up."

"But I don't get it, Sean," Jeff said, still agitated. "It's not fair for them to say one thing one minute and something else the next. It's not right." His voice reached a hysterical pitch. "How can they be so mean?"

"Hush, Jeff," Sean said harshly. "The baby is their flesh and blood. They're human beings, and they have feelings too. In the end, they decided it's better for them to put their differences aside in favor of raising their own child themselves."

The tears that welled in Jeff's eyes spilled over. "I wanted"—he paused to gasp—"I wanted a baby, Sean. I wanted Liam so bad."

"I know you did, Tiger," Sean said. He ran his hand down Jeff's back, caressing him gently.

"You wanted him too," Jeff said.

Sean didn't answer, just continued his caresses of Jeff's lower back until Jeff pulled back.

"You did, didn't you?" Tears oozed down Jeff's cheeks, and he stared into Sean's eyes.

"Jeff, listen," Sean said at last, "we're not taking in my brother's baby. That's all there is to it."

Jeff gasped as though he'd been hit, and he pulled out of Sean's arms. He turned and flung the back door open and fled down the steps.

Sean followed him to the door and watched as Jeff walked through the yard. He wanted to follow and make things all right, but something held him back. It was apparent that the loss of the child had affected Jeff far more than it affected him, and he wanted to give Jeff his space to come to terms with it.

When Jeff reached the end of the yard and tripped over a tree root, Sean snapped from inaction and hurried out into the yard. Dakotah raced past him, and by the time Sean reached Jeff's side, the dog was in his lap, licking his face.

"You don't get to take care of a baby, Kotah, and I don't get to either." Jeff's voice cracked with his crying. "I know you wanted to, but... I don't know what we're going to do now."

Sean stopped. He knew that Jeff could sense him standing there, but Jeff continued to talk to the dog instead of directly to him.

"I don't belong here anymore, Kotah," Jeff continued. "Everyone has a reason for being here except me, and I'm just a burden. Maybe Jesse's right, maybe Sean doesn't really need me or want me anymore."

Those words snapped the spell, and Sean sank down to his knees and pulled Jeff into his lap. Dakotah yelped once and then squirmed out from between them.

"I don't just need you, Jeff," Sean said, his words almost a growl. "I want you. I love you so much, and we don't need a baby to prove that love." He turned Jeff to face him and tucked him in close against him.

Jeff reached up and scrubbed a hand over his face. "But I don't have a reason for being here, Sean. You have a job. Everyone has a job but me. All I do is keep your house clean, but you could hire someone to do that. Someone who wouldn't be in your hair all the time."

"Stop, Tiger," Sean said. "I don't need you to keep the house. I need you here because you bring me happiness. You are changing so much, turning into your own man. I see it, and Gabe sees it too. You don't need a baby to give your life purpose, but if you want a purpose, then let's make you one. There's any number of things you can do to give your life meaning."

As Sean held him, Jeff began to settle. At last he sniffled and said, "Like what?"

Sean was silent for a bit, and then he said, "You're an artist in the kitchen, Jeff. You make things like that pie you made me yesterday, and you don't even think twice about it. You could be a personal chef, or cater parties."

"I don't know," Jeff said softly.

"I do," Sean said. "Jeff, you can do anything you set your mind to."

After a short silence, Jeff said, "But I wanted a baby, Sean."

"I know you did," Sean said.

It was fully light now, and soon Sean would have to shower and struggle through a day of work with no sleep. The cold of the outside air began to settle around them, and Jeff shivered. He stood and waited for Sean to stand beside him, and then together they walked into the house.

Chapter 20

Isolated by a Deed

IN THE days that followed Shannon's early morning phone call, Jeff seemed to retreat. Sean brought him information about a culinary school that would accept him mid-year, but Jeff adamantly refused. An argument ensued when Jeff insisted he wasn't reading well enough to go to school because Sean disputed that and said he was. Eventually they called a truce when Jeff promised to see about enrolling when the new school year started and that he would concentrate on getting his GED instead.

Sean began to throw himself headlong into his work. His personality was such that he embraced the things he felt passionate about wholeheartedly. Before Jeff, that had been his work, and it wasn't uncommon for him to spend hours of overtime on the intricacies of contracts his firm negotiated. After Jeff came along, his energy and passion had transferred over to building their relationship. Now it began to veer back to his work, and many times he came home very late.

On this particular night, Sean had brought his work home with him. He had been distracted at dinner and missed the fact that Jeff said he was trying a new recipe and wanted Sean's opinion on it. After the meal, Sean had retreated to his office to work on the contract again, and it was past midnight when he finally shut down his computer and headed to bed.

As he came through the doorway, he stopped short and gasped. Despite the late hour, Jeff was still awake. He was propped against the headboard of the bed, his hair loose on his shoulders. The sheet was draped low across his hips, and even from the doorway Sean could see that he was naked. He oozed sensuality, and once Sean recovered from the shock, he walked slowly toward the bed, almost as though he were being pulled on the string of Jeff's desire.

"You didn't need to wait up for me, Jeff," Sean murmured when he reached the bed.

"Yeah, I did," Jeff said. He shifted closer, and the sheet pulled away from his hip. He rolled on to his belly and looked up at Sean through the curtain of his hair. "Make love to me, Sean."

A stifled groan gathered in the back of Sean's throat as he unbuckled his belt and opened his pants. "Been a long time, Jeff," he murmured. He continued to undress as he watched Jeff roll back to his original position.

"Too long," Jeff said.

Fully undressed, Sean climbed up on the bed and moved close to Jeff. As he bent forward to nuzzle against Jeff's lips and gently cup his erection, he was assailed with the scent of the sandalwood soap Jeff still used. "You feel good, Tiger," he whispered against Jeff's lips.

Jeff moaned in answer and slid his hand down Sean's hip. He eased closer and gave himself fully to the heady kisses, giving a small gasping moan when Sean wrapped his hand around both of their cocks together and stroked gently. "Love me, Sean."

"I do love you, Jeff," Sean murmured. He pinned Jeff's leg between his own as he continued to stroke him. "Love you so much."

Jeff moaned and arched against Sean. He spread his legs when Sean rolled between them. He raised both arms and looped them up around Sean's neck.

Absently, Sean reached for the lube. Too much work and not enough sleep, plus the knowledge that it had been too long, set him on autopilot. He thrust his fingers inside Jeff's passage and moved his kisses down Jeff's neck. He shuddered as his cock dragged against Jeff's leg. Quickly, he rose up on his knees, reached for a condom, and tore the packet open. He looked down at Jeff through hooded eyes and murmured, "So fucking hot…."

"I'm yours, Sean," Jeff said, and he raised his arms above his head and arched up.

Sean lifted Jeff's legs, guided them up over his shoulders, and with no further preparation, he pushed inside him hard.

Jeff gasped, and his hands clenched into fists. He rolled his head to the side on the pillow and whimpered.

"Shit," Sean groaned, realizing that he had not spent enough time preparing Jeff. He bent as close as he could and cupped the side of Jeff's face, urging him to turn his head. "Jeffrey," he breathed.

Instead of easing, Jeff clenched his hands tighter, kept his eyes squeezed shut, and barely stifled another whimper.

Sean feared that pulling away would be worse than staying where he was. He turned and pressed his lips against Jeff's calf, then reached for the lube again. He squeezed a dollop along the length of Jeff's cock and began to stroke him.

Jeff kept his face turned away, his breathing coming in short gasps. His body responded even though it was quite clear his soul was hurt. Before long he erupted through Sean's fist, and only then did he unclench his fists and begin to relax tight muscles. He kept his face turned away.

Moving his hips in a gentle rocking motion, Sean realized that pulling away now would only be an admission of guilt. Although he did feel guilty, he didn't want to bring that emotion to their bed, so once Jeff relaxed, he thrust inside him until he came, though he took no pleasure from it. When he pulled out, Jeff rolled away from him and curled into a ball. Sean itched to reach out and touch him, but he kept his distance. He left the bed long enough to go and remove the condom.

When he returned, Jeff had pulled the covers up over himself and had moved to the far edge of the bed. Sean caught his lower lip between his teeth, then turned off the light and got into the bed. He reached across the open space between them but stopped short of touching Jeff. Sleep eluded him, and he strained his eyes and ears through the darkness until he heard Jeff sniffle. He sighed and rolled over to face the wall.

The next morning, Sean got up early, showered, and left without saying anything to Jeff. Jeff remained in bed late as sleep finally caught up with him. When he finally got up, he spent a long time in the shower letting the hot water pelt over his body.

Fearing he would fall into despair, he spent the day in the kitchen making Sean's favorite dinner. When he heard Sean's SUV in the driveway, he left the lasagna cooking in the oven and went out to the living room. He sat on the couch and picked up a magazine, hoping he looked casual, as if nothing was wrong.

"Jeff?"

Jeff's hands tightened on the magazine, and he looked up and gasped. Sean stood just inside the archway between the kitchen and the living room, a soft white teddy bear with a pink ribbon around its neck in his hands. It looked incongruous against his tailored business suit, crisp white shirt, and red necktie.

Holding the bear in front of him like a shield or the peace offering it was meant to be, Sean advanced across the room and sat beside Jeff on the couch. He reached over and set the bear in Jeff's lap.

"What's this?" Jeff said, his voice cracking with emotion.

"I went to the arcade today at lunch, threw some balls at a target. I guess…." He sighed and reached up to run a hand through his hair. "I knocked all the targets down."

Shivering at the intensity in Sean's look and the admission that he had thrown the ball hard enough to knock all the targets down, Jeff hugged the bear against him.

"I'm sorry, Tiger," Sean murmured.

Jeff buried his face against the bear as unbidden tears welled in his eyes. Finally, his voice muffled, he said, "I don't want to talk about it."

"But we have to, Jeff," Sean said, and he reached over and urged Jeff closer, wrapping an arm around him. "If we ignore it, then it will just fester. I hurt you, and that's something I never wanted to do."

Leaning in against Sean and breathing in his familiar scent while still clutching the bear, Jeff said, "It's okay, Sean. I know you didn't mean to."

"Whether I meant to or not isn't the issue," Sean said, and he bent down to kiss the top of Jeff's head. "I allowed myself to get distracted… and I was tired."

"You're tired because you work so much," Jeff said, and then he gasped. "I mean—"

Sean was silent for a bit, and then he said, "You're right. I have been working too much, and I guess it's because I still don't know how you feel about us, now that we're not going to have a kid." He tightened his arm around Jeff and kept him from struggling away. "I don't know because instead of asking you, I've been avoiding you. It's wrong, but sometimes it's easier to sweep things under the rug to avoid a confrontation."

When Sean tightened his hold, Jeff relaxed against him and listened. "Do you still want me, Sean?"

"I want you," Sean said. "I love you."

"Whenever Hunter hurt me, he called me Jeffrey," Jeff whispered.

"Oh, Tiger," Sean said, and he reached down to tip Jeff's face up. "I'm sorry."

The timer dinged in the kitchen, and this time Sean allowed Jeff to pull away. He handed the teddy bear to Sean and turned to walk into the kitchen.

Remaining on the couch, Sean squeezed the teddy bear, a cold knot in the pit of his belly. It was a wonder he hadn't totally given into his baser instincts the night before and flipped Jeff over to violate him on his knees the way Hunter had. He bit his lip as the coldness spread, and he vowed to himself that things would change. They would have to if he intended to salvage what was between him and Jeff.

Chapter 21

Now My Ladder Is Gone

THINGS eased slightly between Jeff and Sean after they skirted around the issues between them. Jeff acknowledged to himself that the attempt at talking about things that bothered him was a good start, but in the back of his head, he could imagine Gabriel gently reminding him that it hadn't been enough.

Sean had eased off his work schedule and came home on time more often. Many nights after dinner, they huddled together on the couch and watched old movies. Sometimes they talked about the events of their days, but usually they sat in silence.

Lovemaking tapered off, but on the rare occasions when they did indulge, Sean rigidly controlled himself, leaving them both aware that things were different between them. The spontaneity was gone, and while there was gentleness, the spark had dimmed. It hadn't been doused entirely, but neither was willing to take the bull by the horns.

Jeff moved slowly around the kitchen, cleaning up the breakfast dishes. He had had a pain in his belly since the middle of the night, and as a result, he hadn't eaten any of his pancakes. "Are you going to be able to help Luke today? He should be here soon."

A frown puckered between Sean's brows, and he looked up from his newspaper. "Luke's coming over?"

"I told you last week," Jeff said. "There was a plant sale at the college where he works. He got a bunch of roses to plant in the yard."

"Luke doesn't need my help with that," Sean said as he folded the paper. "He's a whiz with that kind of stuff. Besides, there's a game on I was going to watch."

Jeff sighed and pressed his hand against his side. "I just thought it would be nice, all of us in the yard for a change."

Sean pushed back from the table. "Tell you what, I'll come out there at halftime and see if he needs help, deal?"

"I guess," Jeff said. He draped the dishtowel over the rack.

Sean dropped a light kiss on the top of Jeff's head and went into the living room. He flipped on the TV, and just as the pre-game activities were getting started, his phone rang. With a frown of puzzlement when he saw the caller ID, he said, "Hey, Andy, what's shakin'?"

"Not much, Sean, you?"

"Something tells me there's a reason for your call," Sean said. "I mean, I get it, we put all the bullshit in the past, but you haven't been tearing down my door since that day in the park, so what's up?"

"Never one to let any grass grow under your feet, were you, Sean?" Andy said with a chuckle. "But now that you bring it up, there was something I wanted to ask."

"What's that?" Sean set his chair to recline, half his attention on the kickoff.

"It's been over a month since I gave you that paperwork to fill out. I know it ain't none of my business, and I know you're not adopting the kid anymore, but you still planning to go through with the domestic partnership?"

Sean stirred restlessly in his chair, then said under his breath, "It's going to be hard. Jeff doesn't have a job, so I can't put him on my house deed, and he doesn't drive, so it's no use putting him on the car title."

"There's ways around that shit, though, Sean, I told you that already. Get him a life insurance policy and set yourself up as beneficiary, then amend your own policy. Hell, even open a joint credit card. The state only needs two documents of proof," Andy said.

"I don't know, Andy," Sean said.

"You still love him, don't you? He's still living there. Must be something between the two of you."

"Yeah, yeah… I still love him." Sean kept his eyes glued to the TV screen. "Just not in a hurry anymore."

"Why not?" Andy prodded.

"Why the fuck is it any of your business anyway?" Sean said irritably.

"Look, Sean, in the grand scheme of things, anyone here at the firm could have drawn the documents up for you, and so technically I guess you're right, it ain't none of my business," Andy said.

"Okay, Andy, I get it, and if your goal in calling me was to piss me off, then mission accomplished." Sean shifted irritably in his chair.

"Peace, bro. At the end of the day, I don't give a shit. It's your life, after all," Andy said. "All I'm saying is that Jeff seems like a great kid, and you've been a sight more settled down since he came into your life. Maybe it's time to pull your head out of your ass and re-evaluate things a bit." There was a silence, and then he said, "You made this my business by even suggesting it, but did you ever have that talk with him?"

"What talk?" Sean said.

"Don't be obtuse, Sean. You know what I'm talking about. You know me—I ain't afraid of being crude. I can spell it out if you want."

"Fuck, Andy," Sean growled. "That is where I draw the line."

"Fine," Andy said. "This is all standard operating procedure for you, and I don't know why I bothered. If you want to know the truth, this is exactly the reason why I never call you anymore. I said I wasn't going to make you pay for drawing up the agreement papers, but if you're not going to use them, have the balls to send them back, because ordinarily there is a fee associated with filing them."

After a prolonged silence, Sean said, "If it was anybody else talking to me like this, I'd kick their ass."

"And because it's me?" Andy asked softly.

Sean sighed. "What's that lawyer term? 'I'll take it under…'?"

"Take it under advisement," Andy said. "And Sean, I really wasn't trying to stir up the shit."

Sean sighed again. "Yeah, I know."

Talk was stilted between them after that, and Sean was left wondering what had even prompted Andy to call in the first place. After a while, he lost himself in the game and didn't even hear Luke arrive.

Jeff was waiting when Luke pulled up in the driveway with the rose bushes in the back of his car. Dakotah frisked around his heels as he walked out to meet his brother.

"Hey, munchkin," Luke said. "I got you five different kinds. You know where you want them all?"

Jeff pressed his hand to his side as another pain shot through his stomach. "What kinds did you bring?" Dakotah jumped up on him, and Jeff pushed him away irritably.

"English tea rose, a climbing vine, and because I know you like purple, I got a sterling silver rose. A few hybrids—I think you'll like them because they smell so nice." Luke stooped to pick up Dakotah's ball and tossed it across the yard.

"You know what's best," Jeff said. "Maybe the climbing one by the bedroom window?"

"Sounds like a plan," Luke said with a wink.

Jeff limped across the yard toward the hammock with Dakotah yipping at his heels.

"You okay, Jeff?" Luke called.

"Fine," Jeff called as he settled in the hammock. "Just a little tired."

"Well, lie in the hammock and direct me from there," Luke said. He turned away and whistled as he continued to unload the roses. "I'll put the sterling silver rose over here. It needs a lot of water, and it should get some of the runoff when Sean washes the car."

It was peaceful in the yard, bees buzzing amongst the flowers, Dakotah chasing butterflies, and Luke planting the roses. After a while, Luke noticed that Jeff seemed to have dozed off, and he worked in silence.

When Dakotah tired of the butterflies, he picked up his soggy tennis ball again and deposited it in Jeff's lap. Startled from his light doze, Jeff opened his eyes.

"Okay, Kotah," he said softly. "Just for a little bit." He struggled out of the hammock, and after he took a few steps, he sank down to the grass, clutching his belly. "Fuck."

Luke looked up and sprinted to Jeff's side. "What's wrong, munchkin?" He hugged Jeff close.

"My stomach fucking hurts," Jeff mumbled.

"How long? Was it something you ate?" Luke covered Jeff's hand with his own.

"All day," Jeff gasped. He pushed Luke's hand away. "Didn't eat anything weird."

"You should have said something," Luke said, and he stood. "I'm going to get Sean."

"No," Jeff wailed. "Don't bother him. I'll be okay."

Without answering, Luke stood and ran across the backyard and up the stairs into the kitchen.

Jeff curled up into a ball and mumbled as Dakotah licked his face.

In less than a minute, Sean came bounding down the back steps and across the yard with Luke on his heels. "Jeff, what's wrong, Tiger?"

Tears filled Jeff's eyes. "My stomach."

Sean knelt down and pulled Jeff into his arms, cradled him gently, and kissed the top of his head.

"His belly is distended," Luke said.

"Grab my phone," Sean said over his shoulder. "Gabe's number is in the favorites. Call him."

"No," Jeff protested weakly. "Maybe if I went inside and had some water…."

Luke disappeared back inside the house, and Sean cradled Jeff close. "Shh, Jeff. Gabe can tell us if anything's wrong."

When Luke returned, he said Gabe and Mark were both at the clinic and were expecting them. They piled into Luke's car, and all the way to the clinic, Sean sat in the back seat, holding Jeff tightly. The conversation with Andy still echoed in his brain. He whispered against the top of Jeff's head, "I love you, Tiger."

Jeff was quiet, his face turned in against Sean's shirt. Sean's words were soothing, but they were not enough to take away the fiery pain in his gut. He stiffened and moaned softly. Sean tightened his hold.

Chapter 22

When Things Fall Apart

GABRIEL was waiting by the front door when Sean and Luke arrived at the clinic with Jeff. He directed Sean into one of the exam rooms.

"Luke says it's his stomach," Gabriel said as he washed his hands.

"I guess it's been hurting him all day," Sean said. He stood next to the exam table, keeping his hand firmly on Jeff's back. "I didn't know it was… this bad."

Gabriel dried his hands and came closer. He smoothed a hand over Jeff's brow before he lifted his shirt and eased the waistband of his jeans down far enough to let him prod at Jeff's stomach.

Jeff howled and tried to pull away. Sean braced himself and held Jeff steady.

"Jeff," Gabriel said softly, bending closer, "has it just been hurting today, or is it longer than that?"

"I don't know," Jeff moaned, his eyes squeezed tightly shut, tears leaking from the corners.

"You do know," Gabriel said firmly. "Has it been hurting since last night?"

"Yes," Jeff whispered. "All night long."

Gabriel pressed again, and when he pulled his hand away, he said, "Which hurts worse, when I press on it, or when I take my hand away?"

Jeff's face was tight with pain. "Both," he managed, and he swallowed hard.

"Do you feel sick?" Gabriel asked as he laid his hand on Jeff's brow again.

This time, all Jeff could manage was a nod.

Turning away, Gabriel murmured to Sean, "He's feverish, there's abdominal tenderness and rebound pain, and nausea on top of that. I'll have to take some blood and do an ultrasound, but I think it's his appendix."

"Shit," Sean said, and he reached down to take Jeff's hand. "If it is, will you have to operate?"

"Yes," Gabriel said, "before it ruptures."

Jeff stirred and opened his eyes. "What did you say?"

Sean turned and bent down to brush his lips over Jeff's forehead. "It's your appendix, Tiger."

"You're not—" Jeff struggled against Sean's hold. "You don't mean cut me open, do you?"

A frown creased Gabriel's brow. "It's not a traditional surgery, Jeff. I'll just make three small incisions. You'll be able to go home tomorrow."

"No," Jeff said. "You can't."

"Baby," Sean said, bending down to kiss Jeff's cheek, "it's okay."

With surprising strength, Jeff wrenched himself away. Eyes wide open and wild-looking, he said, "Don't cut me with a knife."

"Hush, Tiger," Sean said. He stepped closer to try to take Jeff in his arms, but Jeff pulled away further. "Jeff?"

"Don't let him cut me open, Sean. Please… don't…." Jeff's voice caught on a sob.

Sean reached forward and pulled Jeff back into his arms. "Gabe will put you to sleep first, Jeff, and you won't feel anything."

"No," Jeff moaned softly. "No knives."

Frowning, Gabriel laid a hand on Jeff's knee. "This is different, Jeff. The incisions are so small they should hardly leave a mark. You have to trust me."

"I don't trust anyone with a knife," Jeff said, and his body stiffened with a mixture of fear and pain.

Gabriel stepped back. "Hold him, Sean."

Mark appeared in the door with a syringe on a tray. As Sean held Jeff tightly, Mark gave him the fast-acting sedative.

"This surgery should be done in the hospital, Sean," Gabriel said, "but since Mark's here, I can manage it here in the clinic. We'll start him on an IV for the pain and add some antibiotics. Has he eaten anything today?"

"Said he wasn't hungry at breakfast, didn't even have any coffee," Sean said.

"Good. That means we can do the surgery in a few hours. Even without the blood work and ultrasound, I'm relatively sure his appendix will have to come out."

"Please," Jeff whispered, "don't let him cut me with a knife, Sean. Promise me."

Sean bent down closer to Jeff. "I can't promise you that, Jeff. If Gabe doesn't operate and your appendix bursts, then—"

Jeff turned away and moaned.

"That's the reason why I don't want to move him to a hospital," Gabriel said.

Sean turned grateful eyes on Gabriel, and he lifted Jeff into his arms, carrying him down to the day surgery clinic. He remained by Jeff's side as the IV was inserted and the blood work was done. By the time Gabriel did the ultrasound, Jeff had slipped into a doze.

The blood work showed the suspected elevation of neutrophils, a kind of white blood cell, and the ultrasound reinforced Gabriel's diagnosis of acute appendicitis.

"It's time," Gabriel said. "Fortunately, it has not ruptured, so we can perform laparoscopic surgery."

Jeff stirred, and his eyes fluttered open. He turned wide eyes on Sean as the nurse prepared to wheel him from pre-op into surgery. "No," he wailed. "Sean, I told you. Don't let him cut me with a knife."

Sean stood helplessly and watched as Jeff was wheeled out of the room.

Luke had remained in the waiting room, and he approached and laid a hand on Sean's back. "Sean," he said, "he's going to be okay."

"I feel like I'm breaking a promise to him," Sean said, running a hand through his hair. "He wanted me to promise I wouldn't let Gabe cut him, and even though I said I couldn't promise tha—" He took a shaky breath. "He counts on me to protect him, Luke."

"You didn't promise him, though," Luke said. "By letting Gabriel do the surgery, you are protecting him. He's got to understand that."

"I don't think he does, though," Sean said as he collapsed into a chair, head in his hands. "Besides, things haven't been that good between us in a while. I hate that he had that on his mind before he went into surgery."

"Things aren't always perfect, Sean," Luke said as he extracted his phone from his pocket. He frowned at the screen, and with a sigh, he put the phone away. "I sent Jesse a text."

"What?" Sean said, a tinge of anger in his voice.

"He had a right to know," Luke said.

"Fuck," Sean said.

"Jesse's a prick most of the time," Luke said with a sigh. "He's got a misplaced sense of machismo when it comes to me and Jeff." He was quiet for a moment before he said, "I just wish he...."

"Wish he had some human decency?" Sean said softly.

"Yeah," Luke said.

"I wish I had that too," Sean whispered.

"You do, Sean," Luke said. "You love Jeff. You'll get through this."

They fell into silence, and before much longer, Gabriel came to tell them that the surgery had been a success.

"His appendix was swollen. Looks like we caught it in time. He's still under, but in about half an hour, you can go and see him. He'll have to stay overnight, but I have the staff for that."

"Thanks, Gabe, for everything. I know this was short notice, and now you have to pay extra staff, and...." Sean's voice trailed off.

"No worries, Sean," Gabriel said. "You know I'd do anything for you."

"I know," Sean said.

Jeff was stirring by the time Gabriel let Sean and Luke see him. His eyes were unfocused, and he closed them as soon as Sean took his hand. He struggled and tried to pull away.

"Whoa, Jeff," Sean said. "Settle down. I'm not going to hurt you."

"What happened?" Jeff croaked.

"You had your appendix out," Sean said as he stroked Jeff's brow.

Jeff's eyes flew open, and he pulled away from Sean again. "Fuck," he muttered. "You lied to me. You promised you wouldn't—" His voice died away on a wail of pain.

"Lie still," Sean said, and he reached up to pin Jeff against the bed. "You'll pull the stitches."

"You cut me," Jeff moaned.

"Jeff, listen to me," Gabriel said firmly. "There was no other option. Your appendix had not ruptured, but I had to take it out before it did. I made three small incisions. They'll heal up to nothing."

"I said no knives," Jeff said, his voice catching on a sob. "I can't believe you let him do it." He writhed, obviously still in pain.

"The pain will ease," Gabriel said, "but if you don't lie still, I'll have to tie you to the bed. You don't want that."

"I didn't want you to cut me either," Jeff said, and he broke down into tears.

Sean stood back, a helpless look on his face.

"Let me talk to him alone," Luke said, and when the others had gone, he reached up and took Jeff's hand. "What's wrong, munchkin?"

"They cut me," Jeff said petulantly, tears still oozing down his cheeks.

"They had to cut you, Jeff, or your appendix would have burst. Do you know what that means?" Luke asked.

"I don't care what it means," Jeff replied.

Luke reached up calmly and stroked Jeff's brow. "When an appendix ruptures, it sends germs spreading through your body. If Gabriel hadn't operated, you would have died."

"I told him not to touch me with a knife," Jeff said as he turned his head restlessly on the pillow, "but he did. And Sean let him. And now it's more scars, Luke. More marks on my body."

"And every one is a battle scar, a mark of courage that you've withstood more than the average man could take, and you survived." Luke spoke softly, caressing Jeff's forehead tenderly. "Be they meaningless letters on your hip or surgery scars, they don't change you, Jeff."

Jeff snorted. "Hardly meaningless letters, Luke." He swallowed hard against another moan of pain. "They represent Hunter's mark on me."

"Or," Luke said, "they could represent happiness, harmony, heaven, and health." He stood and looked idly at the bag hanging on Jeff's IV pole. "You should think about what you said to Sean and Gabriel. They've done a lot for you, Jeff, and you said some hurtful things. Sean nearly paced a hole in the floor waiting for you, and Gabriel did the surgery here in his clinic so you didn't have to go to a hospital." Frowning, Luke bent forward to read the tag on the IV bag. Then he turned back to look at Jeff. "You should think about apologizing to them."

Jeff closed his eyes, and when he spoke again, his voice was slurred. "I don't feel very good, Luke."

"I know, munchkin," Luke said. "I'm going to go talk to Gabriel about that now. You'll feel better soon."

Luke found Sean sitting slouched in a chair in Gabriel's office, his hand over his face. Gabriel sat behind his desk, chin on his hand. Both looked exhausted and defeated.

"Gabriel?" Luke said as he eased into the room. "You're giving Jeff Demerol?"

"Standard procedure," Gabriel murmured, "giving a strong pain med after surgery."

"I know," Luke said, "but did you know that Jeff was once addicted to heroin?"

"Heroin?" Sean said, sitting up straight in his chair. "When he said he did drugs, I thought he meant he smoked pot."

"Yeah, he mostly smoked pot," Luke said, his fingers twisting together, "but there at the end, Hunter had him hooked on heroin too. It wasn't for very long, but—"

"Long enough that Demerol has no effect," Gabriel said as he stood. "I'll go and change the IV. He must be in an incredible amount of pain." At the door, he turned back and said softly, "Go home, Sean. Get cleaned up; fix yourself something to eat. I'll call you if there's any change, and you are welcome to come back and stay the night if you want." He hurried away to change Jeff's medication.

"Come on," Luke said. "Let me drive you home."

"Fuck," Sean muttered as he stood.

"It'll be okay, Sean," Luke said. "Just wait and see.

As Sean followed Luke out of the clinic, he couldn't help but wonder.

Chapter 23

Bridging the Gap

ONCE the pain medication was changed, Jeff slipped into what was first a fitful sleep, and then eventually, as his body gave in to being pain-free for the first time in two days, he settled into a deep sleep. The day-surgery ward was dark, and Jeff was the only occupant. Gabriel opted to stay even though any of the nurses on his staff would have willingly spent the night looking over the patient. Reasoning that when Sean returned, he would be able to take a break and have a bite to eat, Gabriel checked Jeff's vitals and then went to sit at the desk. He checked his e-mail as he settled into the comfortable silence.

As time passed, it began to register with him that Sean was not coming back. Gabriel tried to call him and got no answer. He rose from his seat and went to check on Jeff, again finding that he was sound asleep. As he stood at Jeff's bedside, contemplating whether or not to call for a pizza, he heard the front door of the clinic opening off in the distance. He went to investigate and found Mark re-locking the door.

"Mark?" Gabriel said.

"Thought you might be hungry." Mark carried a bag of Chinese take-out containers, and he smiled as he walked toward Gabriel.

"You didn't think Sean would be here instead of me?" Gabriel teased.

"Murphy?" Mark snorted. "You know he's the first to run for cover when things don't go according to plan."

They walked back toward the day-surgery ward, and as Mark set the bag on the desk and pulled up another chair, Gabriel cleared space and pulled a stack of napkins from a drawer.

"But this is different," Gabriel said. "Sure, Sean likes things neat and orderly in his life, but that all began to change when he took Jeff in."

Mark pushed one box and a set of chopsticks toward Gabriel and took another for himself. He shrugged. "You know him better than I do, but there was something about the set of his shoulders when he left that clued me in that he was done for the night."

Gabriel split the chopsticks and picked out a broccoli spear. He ate in silence and then reached for Mark's box to grab a bite of noodles. "Even if he had come back, I'd still be here for the night."

"You like the kid, don't you?" Mark said. He slid his chair back and took two cans of soda from the small fridge behind the nurse's station.

"Jeff?" Gabriel nodded. "Yeah, he's a good kid. I just hope Sean pulls his head out and realizes how good Jeff has been for him."

Mark grinned as he skewered a spear of broccoli. "He'll come to his senses."

They ate in silence, each with their own thoughts. When both boxes were empty, Gabriel picked up his soda and sat back in his chair.

"Speaking of pulling a head out," Mark murmured. He collected the boxes and rolled back to toss them into the garbage bin.

Gabriel arched a brow. "Mmm?"

Mark rolled his chair back. He reached up to turn off one of the desk lamps, leaving them bathed only in the glow from the computer screen. From where they sat, either could easily see Jeff, but it was clear he was doing fine and would come through the procedure easily. Mark's knee touched Gabriel's.

"Been doing some thinking," Mark said.

"About?" Gabriel said as he set his empty can on the desk.

"Lots of things," Mark said, "but mainly about you and me." He held up his hand to keep Gabriel from saying anything. "Let me say it, Gabe, and then you can comment."

Gabriel moved his chair so that they were sitting knee to knee, face to face. There would be no hiding from the truth.

"Through the lens of experience, I understand why things happened the way they did ten years ago," Mark said softly. "Back then, I was angry and hurt that you'd leave me in the dust, dash all the plans we made. But now, I realize I was stupid to ever believe that you'd sit on your thumbs for a whole year and wait for me."

"Mark—" Gabriel said, but he fell silent when Mark leaned forward and laid a hand on his knee.

"I get it, Gabe," Mark said. "What we had back then was something special. I would have promised you anything you wanted when we lay there in bed, still tingling from the most incredible sex of our lives. And just like you, I'd have thought better of harebrained schemes when I was alone." He paused and bit his lower lip. "What I'm trying to say is that I was wrong to believe the things you said."

"I was wrong to say them," Gabriel said, but he fell silent when Mark squeezed his knee.

"All that is in the past, Gabe," Mark said. "Indiscretions of youth. It didn't kill us. It made us stronger." He leaned closer, his eyes locked on Gabriel's eyes. "You said you were ready, and now I'm telling you that I'm ready too."

Gabriel reached up, cupped his hand around the back of Mark's neck, and ran his thumb along his cheek. "Ready for me?" he whispered.

As if drawn on a string, Mark bent closer and touched his lips to Gabriel's. Meant only to be a sign of acquiescence, it turned into a deep kiss full of all the longing each had kept for the other over the years. Their bodies twisted as close together as the chairs allowed.

Across the room, Jeff sighed and stirred, breaking Gabriel and Mark apart. He settled again, leaving the men wide-eyed as they looked at one another.

"This isn't the end of it," Gabriel said breathlessly.

"No, it isn't the end," Mark said as he pushed his chair back. "It's a beginning."

For the rest of the night, they kept their distance while being highly aware of one another. Eventually Mark laid his head on the desk, and as Gabriel kept watch over him, his desire grew.

When morning came, Gabriel brewed coffee as Mark stretched himself awake.

"Sorry, Gabe," Mark mumbled. "You'd think I'd be better trained to keep awake."

Gabriel set a mug of coffee in front of him and smiled. "Release of tension will do that to you." He rounded the desk and went to check on Jeff.

Mark took up his mug and said softly, "It's almost seven thirty. Want me to call Sean?"

"Don't bother," Gabriel said as he checked Jeff's blood pressure. Recording the results and leaving the chart at Jeff's bedside, Gabriel turned and walked back. "I tried half an hour ago, and there was no answer." He smiled ruefully. "As much as I'd like to take you home so we could continue our conversation, I'm going to have to ask you to stay here with Jeff while I go and see what the hell is up with Sean."

"I'll agree on one condition," Mark said as he stood and rounded the desk.

"I know your condition, Mark," Gabriel said, "and believe me, I accept it wholeheartedly." He glanced over his shoulder at Jeff and found he was still sleeping peacefully. Before turning back, he reached out and pulled Mark closer, then turned and kissed him. "I won't be long."

Mark pulled back and kissed Gabriel's cheek. "You better not be."

SEAN'S SUV was pulled up in the driveway, but the house was dark when Gabriel arrived. He knocked several times before the door opened a crack. Pushing the door open, Gabriel watched as Sean returned to his chair without making eye contact.

"Hey," Gabriel said. He stepped inside and pulled the door closed behind him. Walking closer, he found Sean disheveled, still wearing the clothes he had worn the previous day. His eyes were red-rimmed as though he hadn't gotten much sleep, and a bottle of bourbon stood open on the table beside his chair. "How much have you had to drink?"

Sean stirred and looked up at Gabriel. "Not as much as it looks like."

"Did you eat anything?" Gabriel asked as he dragged an ottoman closer and sat down facing Sean.

"What is this, the Spanish Inquisition?" Sean growled.

"No, Sean, this is your best friend asking you what the fuck is up? I called you half a dozen times, and you didn't answer. Your mate is in the hospital, and you're home drinking. What gives?"

With a sigh of irritation, Sean turned away.

Gabriel leaned in closer. "Don't look away from me, Sean." An edge of anger entered his voice. "It's not like you to run away from responsibility, so what the hell would you call this?"

"'This' isn't anything, Gabe," Sean said. "It's me thinking."

"Bullshit, Sean. It's you hiding. It's you convincing yourself of things that aren't true. A man with any decency would have come back to the clinic last night, not stayed holed up at home drinking himself into a stupor." Gabriel's usually pleasant face was covered in hard lines.

Sean turned back and blinked. "Whoa, where the fuck did all the animosity come from?"

"You, Sean. It comes from you. Don't tell me—let me guess. While you sat here 'thinking' last night, you convinced yourself that it's too much trouble or too much work to have Jeff in your life anymore. You decided that this is the end, and you're going to throw everything you've worked for over the last year down the drain because this hurt your psyche too much." He paused, and his voice took on a mincing tone. "It's too hard."

"Fuck you, Romano," Sean said, his face flushing. "Who the fuck do you think you are?"

"No. Fuck you, Sean Murphy," Gabriel said, his eyes flashing. "Tell me I'm a liar. Tell me there's some other reason why you didn't come back last night."

The flush on Sean's cheeks turned into a beet red stain, and he opened his mouth to shoot back a rejoinder but then deflated and closed his eyes. "You ain't a liar, Gabe."

Gabriel dipped his head and clasped his hands together. "So?"

Sean sighed and reached for his empty glass, set it on edge on the arm of his chair, and turned it slowly. "I don't know what to do, Gabe," he said at last. "All my life I've been in control, been the one calling the shots. Now, with Jeff, I don't… I can't…."

"You're in love, Sean," Gabriel said. "Love is give and take. Love isn't easy. When you love someone, you give up control of a small part of your soul. When they hurt, you hurt. But when they are happy, you are ecstatic." He unclasped his hands and laid one on Sean's knee. "Don't throw all this away because of some macho sense of need to be in control."

The glass flat against the arm of the chair, Sean looked up at Gabriel. "How is he?"

Gabriel smiled. "Sleeping for now, but he'll wake up soon." He squeezed Sean's knee, then let go and sat back. "Take a shower, get some breakfast, and then come over to the clinic. I want to keep him in another night, but I'm sure he'll want to see you. Besides, I'm not giving you a choice this time. I want you to spend the night in the clinic with him."

Sean nodded and set his glass aside. "Thanks for staying with him last night," he said softly.

"I wasn't alone," Gabriel said, "but that's why I can't stay tonight."

"You lost me," Sean said, cocking his head to the side.

"Mark kept me company," Gabriel said with a wink. He stood and turned to leave. "Come as soon as you can."

"I will," Sean said.

Chapter 24

Shining Knight in Armor

WHEN Gabriel returned to the clinic, he found Mark talking to Jeff, and he paused in the doorway to listen to their conversation.

"We had to send him home because he was like a caged bear. Didn't want him scaring the other patients," Mark said, and he winked as he checked Jeff's IV bag. "He'll be back any time now, and he'll be glad to see you're awake."

"Is he mad at me?" Jeff asked.

"Why would he be mad at you?" Mark said.

"I don't know," Jeff murmured, "but I guess I was kind of a baby about the pain. And I think I yelled at him."

"Listen," Mark said, and he pulled up a chair close to Jeff's bed. "There were some things we didn't know, so we gave you the wrong kind of pain medication. Once we figured that out, you settled right down. Having your appendix that close to rupturing must have been excruciating, and I don't know how you stood it so long. If anything, you were the opposite of a baby about it. Most guys would've given up at the first little twinge of pain. You stuck it out for a long time."

"Because," Jeff said with a sigh, "I know a lot about pain, and I know a lot about keeping quiet about pain."

Mark tipped his head to the side and was quiet for a bit before he responded. "Lots of things happen in the world that shouldn't. Sometimes things have a way of balancing out." He reached up and squeezed Jeff's hand. "When Dr. Romano comes back, we'll take out this IV and get you started on some liquids. You keep those down and there might be a chocolate shake in your future."

Gabriel could see as he stepped through the doorway that tears were welling in Jeff's eyes. He laid his hand on Mark's shoulder. "Hey, Jeff, good to see you awake." Gabriel exchanged a long look with Mark and then said, "You ready to get that IV out?"

"Will it hurt?" Jeff asked.

"It might," Gabriel said, "but you just got done telling Dr. Campana that you can handle the pain because you're tough."

Together, Gabriel and Mark worked on removing the IV and taping up Jeff's arm, and then Mark went to heat up some broth for him.

Jeff looked up forlornly at Gabriel. "Is Sean coming?"

"He'll be here soon, Jeff," Gabriel said. "I'm going to send you home tomorrow, and Sean will stay here with you tonight."

"Hot chicken broth and cold cranberry juice," Mark said as he returned with a tray.

"Thanks," Jeff mumbled.

"Try some of the broth, Jeff," Gabriel said. "Give me just a moment to talk with Dr. Campana."

Jeff picked up his spoon and nodded.

Gabriel guided Mark to the doorway. "Pretty sweet bedside manner, there, Dr. C."

Mark smiled. "I do my best."

"Jeff's been through a lot," Gabriel said, "and I could tell that you hit the right notes with him."

"I gathered as much, but I didn't need to know the whole sordid tale to see that he needed a pep talk," Mark said with a lopsided smile.

"Listen," Gabriel said, "I'd like to continue that conversation we started in the middle of the night." He arched a brow. "You game?"

Mark tipped his head closer. "Finish the conversation, sure, but I'd like a little more than that, if *you're* game."

Suppressing a shudder, Gabriel dug his keys out of his pocket and deposited them in Mark's hand. "Wait for me."

Gripping the keys and brushing his lips across Gabriel's, Mark whispered, "Don't be long."

Jeff had finished the broth by the time Gabriel returned to his bedside. He sipped the juice as Gabriel busied himself tidying up and making up the bed next to Jeff's. He helped Jeff to the bathroom and then got him settled back in his bed and vowed that Sean would be along any minute. Promising to be within a shout's distance, he went to make a phone call in the main reception area of the clinic. As he finished the call, he saw Sean striding up the front walkway with a huge teddy bear under one arm. Gabriel met him at the door.

"How is he doing?" Sean asked.

"Physically, he's fine. Mentally, he misses you," Gabriel said.

A muscle tensed in Sean's jaw. "Well, I'm here now."

"I'm going to let you go in and see him on your own," Gabriel said. "My nurse, Maddy, will be in later. Don't worry, she won't be here to spy on you, but she'll be just a shout away."

"If I need anything, I'll call you," Sean said.

"I won't be available," Gabriel said, soft color flushing across his cheeks.

"Oh?" Sean said.

"I'll be mending a bridge that was burned years ago," Gabriel said softly.

Understanding dawned, and Sean said, "Mending bridges is tiring work, Gabe, but if the clinic catches on fire, I'm calling you anyway."

"The clinic better not catch on fire, Sean," Gabriel said with a wink. "Jeff's better but not ready for fireworks yet."

Sean grinned. "Cute," he said, "but even I know that."

"Okay, look," Gabriel said, "he'll be ready for solid food tonight. Mark promised him a chocolate shake. You can call for pizza; Angelo's delivers."

"Good luck with that bridge," Sean said, and he turned and started down the hallway to the surgery recovery area.

"You make sure you mend your own," Gabriel said softly.

When Sean rounded the corner, he found Jeff lying on his side, his gown pulled up and the covers pushed down. His head was curled down, and he was gazing at the expanse of skin he had uncovered.

Sucking in his breath, Sean walked closer. "What are you doing, Jeff?" he asked.

"Looking at my new scars," Jeff said, his voice soft and slightly cracked.

"Aww, Tiger," Sean said, and he sank down in the chair, the teddy bear in his lap. "They're just small little marks; once they heal, you'll hardly be able to see them."

"I know," Jeff said, his face still turned away. "I was just thinking how I wish they wouldn't fade away, because they're different."

Sean scooted his chair closer. "How so?"

"They weren't put there in anger, Sean," Jeff said, and he finally raised his head. He bit his lip and said softly, "Are you mad at me?"

"No," Sean said, and he leaned closer, cupping the side of Jeff's face. "I love you, Jeff."

"But you can love someone and still be mad at them," Jeff said, his voice cracking again. "Especially if they put you through hell because—"

Sean reached up and laid his finger across Jeff's lips. "Will you listen while I tell you the truth?"

Jeff's eyes were large and luminous, swimming in tears he fiercely held in check. Not trusting his voice, he nodded.

"I brought your bear," Sean said as he handed it over.

Taking the bear, Jeff whispered, "I'd rather hold you than the bear, Sean, if you're going to tell me the truth."

Toeing out of his shoes, Sean walked around to the other side of the bed and carefully eased himself in against Jeff's back. He looped an arm around his midsection gently and pressed his lips against the back of his neck. "Comfortable?" he asked.

Jeff reached up and laid his hand over Sean's arm and nodded.

"Until you came along, Jeff, I was never serious about anything other than military history, my job, and my battle layouts. The day I met you, something snapped, something changed. The truth is, the first time I saw you I thought for sure that you were being abused or taken advantage of. Usually I wouldn't give a shit about things like that, but there was something different that day. I had a, I don't know, a rushing sensation that I had to get you away from all that."

Relaxing slightly, Jeff caressed a small circle on Sean's arm and listened as he continued to talk.

"At first I didn't want anything more than to just protect you, but over time, that changed. I've never been with anyone like you before. It was all new for me. Not to sound crude, but sex for me was always fucking. With you it changed into something else. I guess you brought out those soft feelings that I tried so hard to keep hidden. Andy was the only one who ever caught glimpses of them, but I was bound and determined to squash it all out of my life."

"Why?" Jeff gasped.

"Because," Sean said, his voice dropping to a husky murmur. "I had this misguided notion that real men don't behave like that. Like softness was something to be mocked." Sean fell quiet for a moment and then said, "I've never talked about this with anyone, Tiger."

Moving slowly, Jeff twisted around until his forehead pressed against Sean's. "Before you, Sean, I didn't know anything about softness either."

"I know, Jeff," Sean said, "and once you told me all about you, I kept myself in check, was gentle with you always. I wanted you to feel safe and protected, and I watched you grow and change."

Jeff took Sean's hand in his, twined their fingers together, and eased them up against his chest, waiting for Sean to continue.

"Somewhere along the way," Sean said, and he took a deep breath, "I started to get restless, and instead of telling you, I started to take it out on you."

The tears in Jeff's eyes welled up and spilled over, but he kept quiet.

"At the core, I love you, Jeff, and I want you," Sean said.

"Go on, Sean," Jeff whispered. "I know there's a but…."

"It's hard to hold back," Sean said, an agonized tone entering his voice. "Sometimes, instead of making love to you, I want to fuck you."

Easing back and squeezing Sean's hand, Jeff said, "Then why don't you?"

"Fear, Jeff," Sean said. "Your fear of pain, my fear of hurting you. Yesterday—"

"That's not the same thing," Jeff said, his face flushed. A hint of anger entered his voice. "Yesterday was wrong, like I didn't have any control over myself. I knew Gabriel wasn't going to cut me like Hunter used to, but I couldn't make my brain stop thinking that." The color eased from his cheeks, and the anger left his voice. "I can take a lot more than you think, Sean. Yeah, I'm afraid of knives, but I'm not afraid of you—in bed."

Sean eased closer, brushed his lips over Jeff's. "One time I hurt you, and I've never forgotten it."

"So that one time drove a wedge between us?" Jeff whispered against Sean's lips.

"Did it?" Sean asked.

"Sean," Jeff said, "I've always thought of you as my shining knight in armor. That's why I drew those pictures of you. I never had any of the things in my life that you gave me, but I always wanted them. I wanted someone to talk to me like I had a brain in my head; you did. I wanted someone to tell me I'm beautiful; you did. I wanted someone to make love to me, and you're the only person who ever has. I don't want what we have to be based on fear or holding back. One time you hurt me, and I was surprised, but it didn't drive a wedge between us. Not to me, anyway."

"Do you know what the key to a good relationship is?" Sean murmured, and he went on before Jeff could answer. "Communication."

"Like what we're doing now?" Jeff asked.

"Exactly," Sean said. "I don't think we're broken. I think we can fix us."

"I love you, Sean," Jeff said.

"I'll always love you, Tiger," Sean said.

Silence fell between them, and with all the tension eased, they both began to feel drowsy. Sean roused himself to pull the cover up over them. Although he knew Jeff needed the sleep more than he did, he couldn't bring himself to leave the bed. Part of him suspected that Jeff would sleep better for being held against his warmth, so Sean twisted their bodies until Jeff spooned against him. They drifted off into a doze, not waking again until the middle of the night.

Chapter 25

Flame

MARK sat cross-legged on the floor, examining a tiny wooden elephant. It was a work of art, complete with miniature ivory tusks. He set it back carefully where he'd found it and picked up a camel next. Gabriel had a crèche displayed on the coffee table in the living room, and aside from the traditional figures at the center, the entire thing was surrounded with a multitude of miniature animals. All of the figures were carved from wood, and it was obvious the crèche display was one Gabriel had been building for years, as the animals appeared to have been added individually. Mark very much doubted that elephants had been on hand for the birth of the baby Jesus.

Soon the front door opened, and Gabriel came in. He advanced across the room and sat on the couch behind Mark.

"This is magical," Mark said as he set a leopard back into its place.

"It's a labor of love," Gabriel murmured. "After I started med school, my parents gave up their day jobs and joined the Peace Corps. They started sending me the animals from every country they visited. After a while, it seemed a shame to just set it up for Christmas, so I left it out."

Mark turned, resting an elbow on his knee. "There's a lot I don't know about you," he said softly.

"There's time to learn," Gabriel said with a crooked smile.

"I could make a pot of tea," Mark said.

"Not thirsty," Gabriel said. "There's something else I'd rather have at the moment."

"What's that?" Mark asked, although his husky whisper gave away that he knew exactly what Gabriel wanted.

"You," Gabriel said, and he stood and held out his hand.

"Jeff?" Mark asked as he stood and took Gabriel's hand.

"He and Sean are snug as bugs in a rug by now," Gabriel said.

Mark stepped into Gabriel's arms and whispered, "I've missed this."

"You won't have to miss it again," Gabriel said. He reached down and tucked a finger under Mark's chin, tipping his face up. He lowered his mouth over Mark's and kissed him, softly at first, until it turned into a breath-stealing kiss.

Mark reached up and looped his arms around Gabriel's neck and swayed against him. He moaned when the kiss broke off naturally, and Gabriel pressed open-mouthed kisses along the column of his neck.

"Come on," Gabriel said, and he tucked Mark's hand in his, turned, and led him from the living room into the bedroom.

The shades were drawn against the mid-day sun, and in the semi-darkness, they undressed. Shoes were pushed under the bed. Shirts and pants were laid over a chair, socks and briefs left on the floor. Each groaned aloud when bare skin pressed against bare skin. Gabriel pulled Mark hard into his arms, and together they tumbled back against the crimson velvet coverlet.

Rolling and twisting, Gabriel pinned Mark against the bed. He propped himself up above him, hair tangling down over his eyes. "You feel good, Mark," he murmured as he bent down to nuzzle over Mark's lips.

"Gabe," Mark moaned. He reached up and laid his hands on Gabriel's ass. "Need you."

"Shh," Gabriel soothed. "It's been a long time."

"I don't—" Mark arched up. "Fuck."

Gabriel shifted so that his knees split Mark's legs, urging them wide open. He rose up on his arms and gazed down into Mark's eyes. "Easy, baby," Gabriel crooned. "There's plenty of time. I'm not going anywhere."

"I know," Mark groaned. He reached up and tangled his fingers through Gabriel's untidy locks. "I just want you right now."

"Damn," Gabriel murmured. "Can't argue with that." He slid back enough to work his hand between their bodies and close it around Mark's length. While stroking firmly, he eased back down and kissed him again.

Mark moaned into the kiss. He kept one hand tangled in Gabriel's hair and reached down with the other to tease against his ass.

Tightening his grip on Mark's erection, Gabriel pulled up and whispered, "If I give in to what you want, then I expect to have it my way later."

"Yes," Mark hissed. "Just don't make me wait anymore, Gabe, please."

Gabriel rose up on his knees. "Christ, Mark, so sexy."

Mark raised his knees and slid down closer to Gabriel. "Fuck me."

With a stifled growl, Gabriel backed away, fumbling in the drawer of the bedside table until he unearthed a condom and a tube of lube. It *had* been a while, he mused as he tore open the foil packet.

Impatient, Mark reached for the condom. He curled up, and as he slid the lubricated ring of rubber down Gabriel's cock, he bent forward and flicked his tongue against Gabriel's nipple.

"Fuck," Gabriel groaned. "Want me to lube your fingers so you can get ready for me?"

Mark eased back down against the bed and held his hand aloft. With a growl, Gabriel shoved Mark's hand aside and squeezed the lube on to his own fingers. With exaggerated gentleness, he circled his finger around the rose of Mark's hole and then pushed two fingers inside in one deep thrust.

Arching up, Mark planted his feet against the bed and howled, "Fuck, yes."

Twisting his fingers deep inside Mark's passage, Gabriel bent down and nuzzled against Mark's lips. "Let me know when you're ready."

Mark groaned and reached down to fist his own cock, his knuckles rubbing against Gabriel's belly.

Growling, Gabriel straightened up, eyes locked on Mark's hand on his own cock. "Tease," he murmured. He eased his fingers free, stretched them, and pushed inside again.

Mark's moan caught in the back of his throat, and his hand stilled momentarily. He forced his eyes open, met Gabriel's burning gaze, and growled, "I'm ready, baby."

Gabriel bent down for another kiss, a deep kiss that they both moaned into, and then he rose up again and withdrew his fingers.

Mark pulled his legs up against his chest as Gabriel guided himself down. Their groans twisted into one as Gabriel pushed against him and then rotated his hips as he sank all the way inside.

"That's it, Gabe," Mark mewled.

Gabriel held himself still, felt Mark's body adjusting to accommodate him. He reached down and cupped Mark's cock up against his belly and slowly slid back, and as he thrust inside again, Mark's cock rode through his hand. Slowly, he picked up the pace until he growled, "Come for me, Mark."

That was the trigger, and Mark wailed as he shot through Gabriel's hand. He released his hold on his leg and clamped a hand around Gabriel's arm as he rode out the release.

Releasing Mark's cock, Gabriel braced his hands against the bed and slammed harder against Mark's ass. When he felt his balls tighten up against his body, he threw back his head and howled with release.

Spent, Gabriel rolled to the side. He shuddered when Mark reached over and rolled the condom off his cock, then watched as Mark left the bed and disappeared into the bathroom. He moaned in pleasure when Mark returned with a warm cloth and bathed both their bodies. After the cloth was tossed aside, Gabriel reached for Mark and snuggled close against him.

"Next time," Gabriel murmured, "I take my time with you."

Mark tucked his head under Gabriel's chin. "I look forward to that." He pressed his lips against the pulse still hammering in Gabriel's neck and whispered, "Will you be offended if I go to sleep?"

"No," Gabriel breathed. "I'm on the edge of sleep too."

"Good," Mark said drowsily. "Then let's sleep, and later you can have me again."

"Mmm," Gabriel said. "Something to look forward to."

They drifted into a satisfied sleep.

Chapter 26

Peace of My Soul

THE next morning, Gabriel and Mark woke twined together under the warm covers. After sleeping most of the previous day, they had woken for a shared meal of eggs and toast before falling back in bed to fulfill Gabriel's promise of taking his time.

Mark rolled against Gabriel and rumbled softly, "Guess we can't stay here all day."

"Mmm," Gabriel husked. "We could, after we see our patient home."

Mark pulled back to meet Gabriel's gaze. "You mean it?"

"The way I see it," Gabriel whispered, "we have a lot of catching up to do. I know it's a Monday, but Karen can call and reschedule our appointments. It isn't as if we cancel them all the time. Everyone's entitled to an emergency now and then."

Mark's full lips quirked up in a smile. "Emergency?"

"If I don't get my fill of you, I'll explode," Gabriel said, and he cocked his head to the side. "That sounds like an emergency, yes?"

Mark smiled. "Yes," he said, and he began to slip from the bed.

Gabriel eased forward, and he clasped a hand around Mark's wrist, held him back from leaving the bed. "Hey," he said softly. "I never stopped loving you, Mark."

"I know," Mark murmured. "I never stopped either." He leaned close for a kiss and said, "But you better let me get up, or we'll never get our patient home."

Gabriel chuckled, released his hold, and watched Mark walk into the bathroom.

SEAN and Jeff dozed in shifts and shared a bowl of soup in the middle of the night. Eventually, Sean slid from the bed at dawn and stretched stiff muscles. He settled in the chair by the bed, assuring Jeff that Gabriel would probably protest if he found them in bed together.

When Gabriel and Mark arrived at the clinic, Sean could see immediately that something had changed. There was something in the way that Gabriel couldn't take his eyes off Mark and in the way that Mark hovered close to Gabriel's side.

"Give yourself at least four weeks, Jeff," Gabriel said as he wrote in Jeff's chart. "Take it easy. Your body will tell you how much it can stand. And don't spend all your time lying in bed. Get up and move around. The more you move, the quicker you'll heal." He turned to look at Sean. "He can start on a regular diet as soon as he can tolerate it."

"When do you want him back?" Sean asked.

"I'll be in touch," Gabriel said. "The stitches will dissolve by themselves. He doesn't have to come back unless there's severe pain or he develops a fever. I'm giving you some physician samples of antibiotics and pain pills. The antibiotics run a ten-day course, and the pain pills are administered PRN."

"Speak English, Romano," Sean groused.

"As needed," Mark supplied. He set the bag of Jeff's clothes on the foot of the bed and kept an eye on Jeff as he dressed.

"Everything good?" Sean asked Gabriel in an undertone as they stood on the other side of the thin curtain.

"I don't know what you mean, Sean," Gabriel said innocently.

"I'm not blind," Sean half-growled. "I see you and Mark making goo-goo eyes at each other."

A faint blush across Gabriel's cheeks was the only indication that Sean's words had hit the mark. He murmured, "Take Jeff home. Be good to him, Sean. I'll call you tomorrow."

With a wolfish grin, Sean winked, and then he turned to help Jeff get settled into a wheelchair.

"Thanks, Gabriel and Dr. Campana," Jeff said. "And I'm sorry that—"

"No apology necessary," Mark said briskly. "And you can call me Mark."

Jeff blushed and dipped his head. Gabriel handed the release paperwork over to Sean, and he and Mark accompanied Jeff and Sean to the parking lot.

"I'll add my thanks," Sean said, "and I'll talk to you tomorrow."

Gabriel and Mark watched as Sean drove from the parking lot, and then they turned toward one another.

"I believe," Mark said, "you made a promise earlier."

Reaching to tuck Mark's hand in with his own, Gabriel said, "Indeed I did."

DAKOTAH ran along the fence barking as Sean pulled up in the driveway. Sean smiled over at Jeff as he shut off the engine. "Let me go contain the beast, and then I can help you inside."

"I missed him," Jeff said.

"I know," Sean said. "He missed you too."

When Sean returned from leading Dakotah into the house, Jeff had already unbuckled his seatbelt and opened the car door. "I feel pretty good," he said as Sean looped an arm around him and led him through the yard.

"Let's keep it that way," Sean said. He kissed Jeff's forehead, and once inside the house, he led Jeff into the bedroom, where Dakotah sat on the foot of the bed, tail thumping happily.

"No, Kotah," Jeff said with a gasp. "You're not supposed to be on the bed!"

"Shh, Tiger," Sean said. "It's okay, I told him to wait there for you." He pulled Jeff against his body, wrapping both arms around his back. "You didn't sleep that well last night. I want you to lie down now and let Kotah take a nap with you." He kissed Jeff's forehead again and murmured, "The more you sleep, the faster you'll get better."

"Gabe said I need to walk," Jeff said, his voice muffled in Sean's shirt.

"You will," Sean said. "I'll take you for a walk every day, but right now I want you to sleep."

Jeff stood docilely as Sean stripped him down to boxers and helped him settle under the covers. Dakotah crept up and settled against Jeff's back with a sigh. Eyelids fluttering, Jeff whispered, "I love you, Sean."

"Love you, too, Jeff," Sean said as he bent down and pressed his lips against Jeff's cheek. "So much."

Although he longed to climb into bed with Jeff and Dakotah, Sean crept from the room and tiredly sank into his chair in the living room. The conversation with Jeff still flitted in the back of his head, and he realized that admissions had been made on both sides, things that should have been said a long time ago. Seeing that Gabriel and Mark had mended a fence had added to the already good feelings he had. Things would work out, and he would make sure they did.

The vibration of the phone against his hip stirred him from a light doze. Frowning, Sean pulled the phone out, and his frown deepened as he recognized the caller ID.

"What the hell do you want?" he said angrily.

"Luke said Jeff had surgery. Just calling to check in on him," Jesse said.

"He had the surgery two days ago. What the fuck have you been waiting for?" Sean growled.

"Waiting to see if you had decency enough to call me first," Jesse replied.

"The day I beat your ass to a pulp, I told you that I'd provide for Jeff. Seems to me you washed your hands of both of us, so I guess you'll be waiting until hell freezes over before I call you to tell you shit," Sean said.

There was a silence, and then Jesse murmured, "I still care about him."

"Bullshit," Sean said forcefully. "No one was stopping you from coming over to the clinic to see him when he was there. You're too late, old man."

"I ain't giving up on him," Jesse said with a hint of anger creeping into his voice.

"I'm not either." As Sean said the words, he realized it was true—he would never give up on Jeff and the life they had built together. "When he's better, I'll let him know you called, but if he doesn't call you within a few weeks, then you have his answer. Now leave us the fuck alone." And before Jesse could respond, Sean ended the call.

By the time he had returned to the bedroom, Jeff was asleep, Dakotah snoring against his back. They looked so comfortable that Sean eased down on the large bed, curled around the two of them, and fell fast asleep.

Chapter 27

Return to Life

NO MATTER how much he thought otherwise, Jeff was a fighter. He rested when he needed to and walked every day. During the first week, Sean stayed home to take care of him, and they talked and shared in a way they never really had before. They built models together until Jeff was able to complete one all on his own. Jeff shared all the drawings in his sketchbook, sometimes breaking down with the memories the pictures evoked. It was good for Sean to see the depth and wealth of emotions Jeff had captured in his soul.

Before returning to work, Sean admonished Jeff to rest during the day and that the chores would keep. Luke came to visit as often as his schedule would allow. Even Gabriel came, joking that he would charge for a house call.

True to his promise, Sean let Jeff know that Jesse had called to check on him. After a short silence, Jeff said he had no desire to talk to him. "You're right, Sean, he's not my dad. He said I made my bed here with you, and I like this bed just fine." They hadn't spoken about it again.

Jeff spent his days practicing reading by looking at a cookbook. He tried several recipes, and when they were met with rave reviews from Sean, he had the incentive to keep it up. Gabriel was visiting one afternoon while Jeff was experimenting in the kitchen. He was so impressed, he called the next day and told Jeff that he was in charge of planning a charitable function for homeless gay youth and asked Jeff if he would be interested in catering it. After nervously agreeing, Jeff spent the rest of the day testing new recipes.

Sean's nose twitched as he came home that night. "Mmm, Tiger, what are you cooking that smells so delicious?"

Jeff turned, drying his hands on a towel, a faint blush covering his cheeks. "Puff pastry with curried shrimp." His hair was tied up on top of his head, out of his face. He handed one of the canapés to Sean. "See if you like it."

Bending forward to take it right from Jeff's fingers, Sean closed his eyes as he ate the mildly spicy shrimp and crunchy pastry. "Wow, that's fucking amazing."

"You think?" Jeff said.

"Hell, yeah! What's the occasion?" Sean eyed the tray, and when Jeff nodded, he picked up another.

"Gabriel called today, and… he wanted to know if I could cater a party thing for this charity thing he's planning." Jeff dipped his head and rearranged the shrimps on the tray.

Although Gabriel had called Sean before he called Jeff, he didn't let that show on his face as he raised his hand for a high five. "That's great news, Jeff!"

"Yeah." Jeff looked up shyly. "They're even going to pay me."

"You're going to be an honest-to-God caterer," Sean said as he picked up another shrimp. "And I'm going to be your number one taste-tester."

With a laugh, Jeff turned away and went back to the sink where he had been washing dishes. It had been almost four weeks since the surgery, and he was finally feeling back to normal.

Sean stood watching him, and he picked up a napkin to brush the crumbs from his fingers. Slowly, he walked up behind Jeff and stood close behind him. He bent down and kissed along the nape of his neck, nosed along his ear, and rested his hands along Jeff's hips. "Can those dishes wait?" he murmured gently.

Jeff shivered, and with shaking hands, he picked up the towel again. "Yeah," he whispered.

"Good," Sean said. He turned Jeff toward him, bent forward for a soft kiss, and reached up to pull the band from Jeff's hair. Pinning Jeff gently against the sink, Sean wrapped both arms around him, kissing him again.

Unable to hold back a moan, Jeff swayed against Sean and reached out to steady himself against Sean's hip. Words he wanted to say would not form in his mouth.

Stepping back, Sean reached for Jeff's hand and walked backward slowly out of the kitchen, guiding Jeff along through the living room to the bedroom. Once there, he pulled him close again and murmured, "It's been a long time, Jeff."

"Too long," Jeff said. "I need you, Sean."

Sean backed toward the bed and sat on the edge, pulling Jeff to stand between his outstretched knees. "Let me see you," he whispered as he reached for the hem of Jeff's shirt.

Jeff raised his arms and allowed Sean to pull his shirt off over his head. He reached forward and braced his hands against Sean's shoulders as Sean unbuttoned his jeans and slowly pushed both jeans and boxers down and off. Shuddering, he closed his eyes as Sean wrapped his hand around his erection. "Sean…."

"Hush, Tiger," Sean murmured, and he drew his hand up from base to tip, bent forward, and pressed his lips against Jeff's chest.

"Oh," Jeff groaned. He bent forward and laid his cheek against the top of Sean's head.

Continuing to stroke, Sean explored with his other hand, smoothing over Jeff's hip and circling the fading scars from the appendectomy. He lowered himself down to press his lips against the head of Jeff's cock.

Tightening both hands on Sean's shoulders, Jeff flinched at the feel of Sean's lips on his cock. "Sean, please," he whispered.

Sean stood, pulling Jeff firmly against him, released his hold on his cock, and tipped Jeff's chin upward to kiss him deeply. He whispered against Jeff's mouth, "Love you." Then he turned and eased Jeff down on the bed. As Jeff pushed himself back against the covers and rested on his side, Sean undressed. Before joining Jeff on the bed, he slid open the drawer on the bedside table and took out lube and a condom.

Although he knew that he didn't have to move slowly, this time Sean wanted to. He wanted to feel every nuance of the pleasure that coursed through Jeff's body, wanted to hear every soft sigh, every ragged moan. Sweeping his hand down, he caressed Jeff's hip, pushed closer so that their cocks rested tightly against one another.

Teasing his tongue against the seam of Jeff's lips, Sean gained entrance as he eased Jeff's leg up and over his hip. Tasting desire in his mouth, Sean teased against the crack of his ass until he pressed against his hole and swallowed Jeff's moan.

Flipping Jeff so that he was on his back, Sean loomed above him, hands planted on the bed on either side of his head. He gazed down, seeing only desire in Jeff's eyes, and lowered himself down for another kiss as he groped for the lube. Sitting up on his knees, Sean watched Jeff as he lubed his fingers, saw the single drop of cum ooze from the tip of his cock, and he bent down to lap it up as he slipped his fingers inside Jeff's passage.

With a prolonged wail, Jeff arched up against the tightness of Sean's fingers inside him. He raised both arms above his head and turned his head against the covers. "I dream about this, Sean, about you and me... like this."

Sean rose up again, his fingers still as he felt Jeff's muscles flutter around him. He picked up the condom and tore the packet open with his teeth. As he slid the condom down, he twisted his fingers and pulled them free.

"Look at me, Jeff," he murmured.

Arms still above his head, Jeff rolled his head back and opened his eyes. He gasped, and another shudder ran through him at the intensity of Sean's gaze.

"Christ," Sean groaned, "you're beautiful."

Tears welled up in Jeff's eyes, and his voice broke as he whispered, "I believe you."

"Oh, Tiger." Sean bent down for another kiss, scissoring his fingers inside Jeff's passage again.

Urgency took over, and Sean rose up, sliding his fingers free. He pushed Jeff's legs up and back, poured one last dollop of lube down against his hole, then positioned the wide head of his cock against him. "I love you," he moaned as he slid inside.

Jeff arched up against Sean and wrapped his legs tightly around him. "Love you," he whispered. "So much."

Moving slowly at first, Sean reached between their bodies to cup Jeff's cock up against his belly. As he picked up the pace, Sean could judge by the escalation of Jeff's moans and the scent of his arousal that he was close. He groaned and turned to press his lips against Jeff's calf. "That's it, Jeff... let go."

As the release swept through him, Jeff fell back on the bed, arms stretched wide, howls of pleasure echoing through the room. Sean paused long enough to take in the sight and then renewed his thrusts until he exploded deep inside Jeff's body, closing his eyes at the intensity. He felt Jeff clutching at his arm when he finally came to a rest, and he turned to kiss the backs of Jeff's fingers before slipping free and easing down beside him.

Forehead to forehead, legs intertwined, they lay together as the tremors died away. Sean groped for Jeff's hand and twined their fingers together, holding them up against his chest. He just managed to slip the condom off and drop it into the dish on the bedside table before they both drifted into a light doze.

It was full dark when they awoke. Sean rose from the bed and pulled Jeff up with him. After yanking the covers back, he settled them both back in bed. Cuddling close, Jeff pressed a kiss against Sean's chest. "I like it when it's dark," Jeff murmured.

"Mmm?" Sean responded. "Why's that?"

"Because I'm not as afraid in the dark," Jeff said.

"Mmm, most people are afraid of the dark," Sean said.

"In the dark," Jeff whispered, "I can't see the things that scare me."

Sean was silent for a moment, and then he murmured, "I don't scare you."

"No," Jeff said, and he tightened his hand on Sean's hip. "Remember when I was in the hospital, and we talked?"

"Mmm-hmm," Sean said.

"Sean, you don't scare me, but my memories do. I trust you, and I always have. I want you to... be yourself and not—" Jeff stopped in frustration.

Sean shifted and rolled over on top of Jeff, pinned him against the bed, and made eye contact through the dark in the room. "Are you sure?"

"Yes," Jeff said with an edge of desperation. "I want to be your equal, Sean."

"Tiger," Sean said, raising his hand to caress Jeff's cheek gently, "you already are. It's not a question of you trying to prove something to me."

"I know, Sean," Jeff whispered. "But I have to prove it to myself. You know that old saying that talk is cheap."

His thumb still circling over Jeff's cheek, Sean said, "Is it that sometimes the anticipation is worse than the act?"

"I don't know what that means," Jeff said.

"It means ever since we talked about it, it's been on your mind. You said you can take it, and now you want to be sure you can."

"Yeah," Jeff said.

"Then I won't make you wait, but I want you to understand, Jeff, that I finally see both sides. That isn't what I need all the time." He swept his hand down and cupped Jeff's ass. "Sometimes I need this." He pressed his lips against Jeff's brow. "Once we start, if you want me to stop, you just tell me."

"You're not a monster, Sean," Jeff whispered.

Sean bent down and kissed Jeff, a soft kiss turning hard. He cupped his hand under Jeff's ass and pulled him up against him while moaning into his mouth. He felt Jeff's cock stirring against his, and he knew that Jeff was not afraid.

"Up," Sean commanded. "On your knees."

With no hesitation, Jeff struggled up and settled on his hands and knees. There were no pleas to set the mirror so that he could see Sean, and his moans were strictly sounds of pleasure.

Slipping totally back into his old ways, and knowing that this would only be an occasional thing with Jeff, Sean took his cock in hand

and smeared the drops of precum on the tip against Jeff's ass. There would always be a part of him that would hold back, and he had never been the kind to equate pleasure with pain, but there was something electrifying about this raw sexuality.

Jeff moaned and dropped down against the bed, his cheek against the rumpled covers. He gripped the sheets tightly and rolled his head to the side to whimper, "It's good, Sean."

Stifling a growl, Sean reached for the discarded lube and slicked himself liberally. He paused long enough to slide a finger into Jeff's still slightly stretched passage and then pressed the head of his cock against him again.

"Love you, Tiger," he murmured, one hand on Jeff's hip, the other steadying the base of his cock.

"Love you, Sean," Jeff mewled. "So much."

With that invitation, Sean sank inside Jeff's passage, head thrown back to howl at the feeling of his skin on Jeff's without the protection of a condom. He rocked in deeply and held his hands tight enough on Jeff's hips to leave a bruise, shuddering with the intensity.

Hands still clutched tightly in the wrinkled sheets, Jeff raised up long enough to wail in pleasure before subsiding back down against the bed. His broken mewls of satisfaction were what gave Sean permission to continue, and he didn't hold back.

One hand tangled in Jeff's hair, the other still held firmly to his hip, Sean pulled back and set a hard pace. His body slapped against Jeff's, and he was only vaguely aware that Jeff reached up to cup his own cock up against his body. All that had passed between them surged up, and even through the wildness, he was able to acknowledge that this was different. Jeff's gasp and the fluttering sensation of his muscles tightening around his cock sent Sean plummeting over the edge. He curled down over Jeff's back and came just as Jeff's orgasm waned.

When the intensity subsided, Sean pulled out and flopped down beside Jeff, turning him to pull him against his chest. It was then that he felt Jeff's tears, and he reached over to turn on the bedside lamp. "Jeff?"

Although tears streamed down his face, Jeff smiled, and he said brokenly, "Thank you, Sean."

"Tiger, did I hurt you?"

"No, Sean," Jeff said, gasping. "You loved me."

"Oh, Jeff," Sean whispered as he eased down and pulled Jeff against him. "I'll always love you."

They fell into silence then, each wrapped in their own thoughts and each knowing that a hidden barrier had been passed. Finally, Sean found Jeff's hand and twined their fingers together. He kissed Jeff's forehead gently, and together they drifted to sleep.

Chapter 28

Treasure

THE sun was warm and bright as Jeff and Sean walked the short distance from their house to the park. Dakotah frisked along ahead of them, stopping every now and then to bat his paw at the blue bandana around his neck. He had been to the groomer the day before, and even though Jeff and Sean liked the decoration, Dakotah apparently did not.

"We should just take it off before he destroys it," Jeff said.

"Leave it," Sean replied. "He looks good like that. Festive."

"Every day is a party for him anyway," Jeff said, "because you keep giving him scraps all the time."

"Just because I want him to be as well fed as I am," Sean said with a laugh. They entered the park, and Sean guided Jeff toward the path that led to the tree where they had first met.

"But he's getting fat," Jeff said.

"I am too," Sean said with a wink.

"No, you're not," Jeff said, and he moved closer and laid his hand on Sean's belly.

As they got closer to the tree, Jeff looked up to find a small group of people clustered there. He looked over at Sean and said, "What are they doing here?"

"Who?" Sean asked, his expression innocent.

"Don't pretend you don't see them," Jeff said. "Gabe, Mark, Luke… and I don't know who that other guy is."

Judging the distance and seeing that Luke had started toward them, Sean dropped the leash and let Dakotah run forward. He stopped and took both of Jeff's hands in his. "They're here because I asked them to be here."

Jeff watched long enough to see Luke grab Dakotah's trailing leash and lead him over to the group by the tree. When he turned back, Sean pulled him into his arms and bent down for a small kiss. "The state of Georgia will never allow us to marry each other, Jeff," Sean murmured, "but if you'll have me today, we can do the next best thing."

Stepping closer, Jeff said, "I gave myself to you under this tree a long time ago, Sean. I don't feel like we need the state to approve."

"We don't need the state to approve, Tiger," Sean said, "but I do this—to honor you."

"Oh, Sean," Jeff said, and tears welled up in his eyes.

"No crying," Sean said as he reached up to brush his thumb below Jeff's eye. "Come on." Together they turned and walked toward the group under the tree.

There were smiles all around, and Luke came forward to envelop Jeff in a bear hug. Dakotah barked, and Jeff bent down to ruffle a hand over his back. "Good thing you got all dressed up, Kotah," Jeff whispered.

"Jeff," Sean said, "this is my friend Andy, the lawyer."

As Jeff stood, he was aware vaguely that Sean's friend Andy the lawyer was also a previous lover. He took Andy's hand, and the look that passed between them spoke volumes. Jeff was grateful to this shadow from Sean's past, the one who had seen the glimpses of Sean's true nature. Andy was accepting, and when that brief moment they shared passed, any awkwardness that might have hampered them vanished.

"Dearly beloved, we are gathered here today," Andy said with a laugh. "But in all seriousness, we're all here today to celebrate Sean and Jeff. There have been a lot of ups and downs, but something told me when I got this paperwork together it would all get filled out and signed." He reached up to clap Sean on the shoulder. "Just glad you didn't get cold feet."

"No fear of that," Sean said softly, his arm firmly around Jeff's shoulders.

"Ordinarily, we could have just met in my office. All this takes is a few signatures," Andy said. "But this way we get to pretend it's a wedding." He reached in his pocket and pulled out a sheaf of papers.

Mark moved closer to Gabriel and took his hand as Andy straightened the papers out and handed them to Sean.

There, with the sunlight dappling through the trees and Dakotah's tail thumping against the ground, Sean signed the domestic partnership agreement and then watched as Jeff signed it too. The men burst into spontaneous applause as Andy took the papers back.

"You may now kiss the groom," Andy said with a grin.

"There's something else first," Sean said, and, still holding Jeff's hand, he reached in his pocket and pulled out a square, brown velvet box. "I still remember the day, Jeff, when I came home and found you looking at these." He flipped the lid of the box open with his thumb. He continued to speak, and his words were spoken directly to Jeff's heart even though he allowed the others to listen. "If ever I were going to get cold feet, that was the day, because it all seemed so overwhelming. Sometimes, though, it's good to be overwhelmed."

The tears that had threatened before spilled over now as Jeff looked at the gleaming silver rings nestled side by side inside the box. He still remembered choosing the Celtic pattern as an homage to Sean's heritage. Reverently, he picked up the larger ring and pressed his lips against it. As he slid it over Sean's finger, he whispered brokenly, "I'm always going to be overwhelmed by your love, Sean, and I wouldn't want it any other way."

Sean wrapped his arms around Jeff and bent to whisper against his lips, "Love you, Tiger," and then he sealed their mouths in a deep kiss. When the emotion of the kiss passed, Sean plucked the smaller ring out of the box and slid it over Jeff's finger, then held his hand up against his chest.

Jeff swayed against Sean and leaned in close against him, reassured by the sound of his steady heartbeat.

"This calls for champagne, but we're in the park, and we can't drink," Andy said.

"Come back to our place," Gabriel said, his hand still twined with Mark's. "I might have a little something planned."

"'Our place'?" Sean asked, arching a brow.

"Yeah, Sean," Mark said. "You aren't the only lucky one in this bunch."

Andy declined the invitation to join them at Gabriel's, claiming he had to get back to work. Luke said he could only stay for a short while, and eventually the gathering whittled down to just the four of them.

Jeff sat on the floor beside Gabriel's nativity display, his hand clenched into a loose fist with his thumb covering the new ring. A glass of sparkling cider sat on the table, but he ignored it. Dakotah sat with his head in Jeff's lap. "I'm too full of bubbles already," Jeff murmured, and Dakotah wagged his tail.

Sean, Gabriel, and Mark sat on the couch behind Jeff, drinking champagne and ribbing each other good-naturedly. Sean couldn't believe that Mr. Neat-Freak Gabriel had allowed the dog into the house.

He was still amazed that Gabriel and Mark had been able to mend the broken fence between them. Gabriel said it was all a matter of maturity, and Mark put in that Gabriel wasn't as much of a neat freak as he looked.

For his part, Jeff was glad that Gabriel and Mark had found happiness together. It was one thing he had always hoped for. In his mind, Gabriel was too special to continue life without a mate. Mark was perfect for Gabriel, Jeff thought. There was enough difference between them that they complemented one another perfectly.

"There's even more to celebrate," Sean said as he topped off his glass. He looked down into Jeff's upturned face. "Can I share the news?"

Jeff reached up to tuck his hair behind his ears, and he smiled as he nodded.

Sean raised his glass. "Jeff and I went over to Le Cordon Bleu in Tucker last week, took a tour. He can enroll in a few casual day classes to see how it goes, but they won't count toward a degree until he enrolls full-time."

"Wow, that's great news!" Gabriel said.

Jeff dipped his head and blushed. "My tutor says I'm getting a lot better at reading. I'm still working on the GED."

"You know, if you need any help with that, you can just let us know," Mark said.

"Thanks," Jeff said, "but Sean's been helping me."

"Yeah, but if you need any real help," Gabriel said with an exaggerated eye roll.

"Shut up, Romano," Sean said, smacking him lightly.

"In all seriousness, though," Gabriel said, "I'm proud of you, Jeff. The kids at the shelter still talk about the fundraiser party. Hell, I'm embarrassed to just be serving cheese and crackers today, but I couldn't have asked you to cater your own celebration."

"It's the best cheese and crackers I've ever eaten, though," Jeff said as he reached for another.

Conversation continued, and eventually things began to wind down. Soon Sean sank down on the floor behind Jeff and nuzzled against his neck. "Been a long day, Tiger," he murmured.

"I disagree," Jeff said softly. "I don't want this day to ever end."

"Best part is yet to come," Sean said as he laid his hand over Jeff's.

Jeff shivered, and Dakotah raised his head to look at Sean.

"Time to go home," Sean murmured.

"Home," Jeff whispered in reply.

WITH Dakotah happily occupied chewing a meaty bone, Sean and Jeff made their way through the twilight of the house to the bedroom. They stood by the bed, fingers twined together.

"Back in the early days, Jeff, you fascinated me," Sean murmured. "In a lot of ways, it surprised me that all I wanted was to spend time talking to you and seeing that smile on your face. I never even considered that one day you'd share my bed, and that should have been the sign that something was different, that I was changing."

Jeff tipped his head to the side. "I never thought about us sleeping together either, or I mean, having sex. Because the sleeping part…." He paused and smiled. "That was one of the things that made me know I could trust you."

Sean reached up and cupped the side of Jeff's face gently. "Now we're a complete package. There's still the sleeping, and there's the talking, there's the being together, and there's the sex."

"Sean," Jeff said, licking suddenly dry lips, "I don't want to sleep or talk right now."

"Good thing," Sean said as he dipped down to brush his lips across Jeff's. "I don't want to do those things right now either."

They had established a balance at long last, and as they moved back to shed their clothes, each knew what the other wanted. Sean settled on the bed first, back against the headboard, legs spread wide. Jeff paused long enough to take a bottle of scented lube from the bedside table and lay it next to a condom within easy reach, and then he eased onto the bed between Sean's legs.

Sean rested his chin on Jeff's shoulder and stroked down the front of his belly. He curled his fist around Jeff's length and stroked upward. Neither spoke as they shared the sensation, and a moan whispered from Jeff's lips.

The fading sun sent one last ray of light through the window, and it glinted off the silver ring on Sean's finger as he tightened his hold on Jeff's length and nipped gently at the juncture of neck and shoulder.

Jeff gripped Sean's arm and turned his head down, giving Sean greater access to his neck, and Sean obliged by kissing him again. Goosebumps rose along Jeff's flesh, and he stirred restlessly.

Twisting their bodies, Sean eased Jeff down against the pillows, settling their bodies so that their cocks rested together. For a long moment, he just gazed into Jeff's eyes, and then he lowered himself down and kissed him, parting Jeff's lips with his tongue and tasting the inside of his mouth.

Jeff wrapped both arms around Sean's back, trailing his hands down over corded muscles to rest against his ass. He arched up against Sean's body, feeling the spark that passed between them.

Although there was a sense of urgency echoed in each of them, Sean continued to take his time. "I want the memory of this day," he whispered against Jeff's chest as he slid down, "imprinted on my soul forever."

Too overwhelmed to speak, Jeff curled his hand around the back of Sean's head. He moaned softly when Sean's lips touched the tip of his cock. He spread his legs wider and curled up to watch as he disappeared inside Sean's warm mouth. Overcome, he closed his eyes and flopped down against the bed.

As he tightened his lips around Jeff's erection, Sean groped for the lube. The spicy scent of vanilla filled the air; he slicked his fingers and began to tease against Jeff's hole. As he circled the ruby tip one last time, Sean slid his finger inside and rose up to ease himself along Jeff's side.

Jeff turned toward Sean, tightened around his finger, and moaned. "Please, Sean."

"Not yet," Sean murmured. "You feel nice." He knew he wouldn't be able to hold out too much longer. With two fingers lodged firmly in Jeff's passage, Sean moved closer and nuzzled at his lips.

Jeff found the condom package and tore it open. With shaking fingers, he slid the condom over Sean's cock, feeling his shiver of anticipation. Moving so that he dislodged Sean's fingers, he raised both legs and eased them up over Sean's shoulders.

Bracing himself against the bed with one hand, Sean guided himself and slowly began to fill Jeff's passage. He reached down and cupped Jeff's cock up against his body and held for a moment until Jeff whimpered with need. Then, answering with his own groan of need, Sean began to move.

With iron will, Sean managed to hold back and feel Jeff's release first, but before long, he came, too, and their moans of pleasure intertwined. He continued to rock against Jeff for as long as possible and then slid in as deep as he was able and waited for Jeff to open his eyes.

"You're mine, Tiger," Sean whispered fervently.

"And you're mine," Jeff replied.

Sean eased down beside Jeff, found and caught his hand up against his chest. He rested his thumb over the ring on Jeff's finger, content and loved.

ROWENA SUDBURY lives in southern California with her husband, son, and their wonderful rescue dog. Her love of reading was born in the fifth grade, and she began writing soon after that. Writing has always been her passion and escape from the real world.

Rowena finds herself thinking through the minds of her characters quite often, to the point that she always has to carry a small journal with her so she can capture their thoughts and weave them into stories when she gets home.

Visit Rowena's blog at http://rowenasudbury.livejournal.com/ and e-mail her at rowenasudbury@gmail.com.

Also by ROWENA SUDBURY

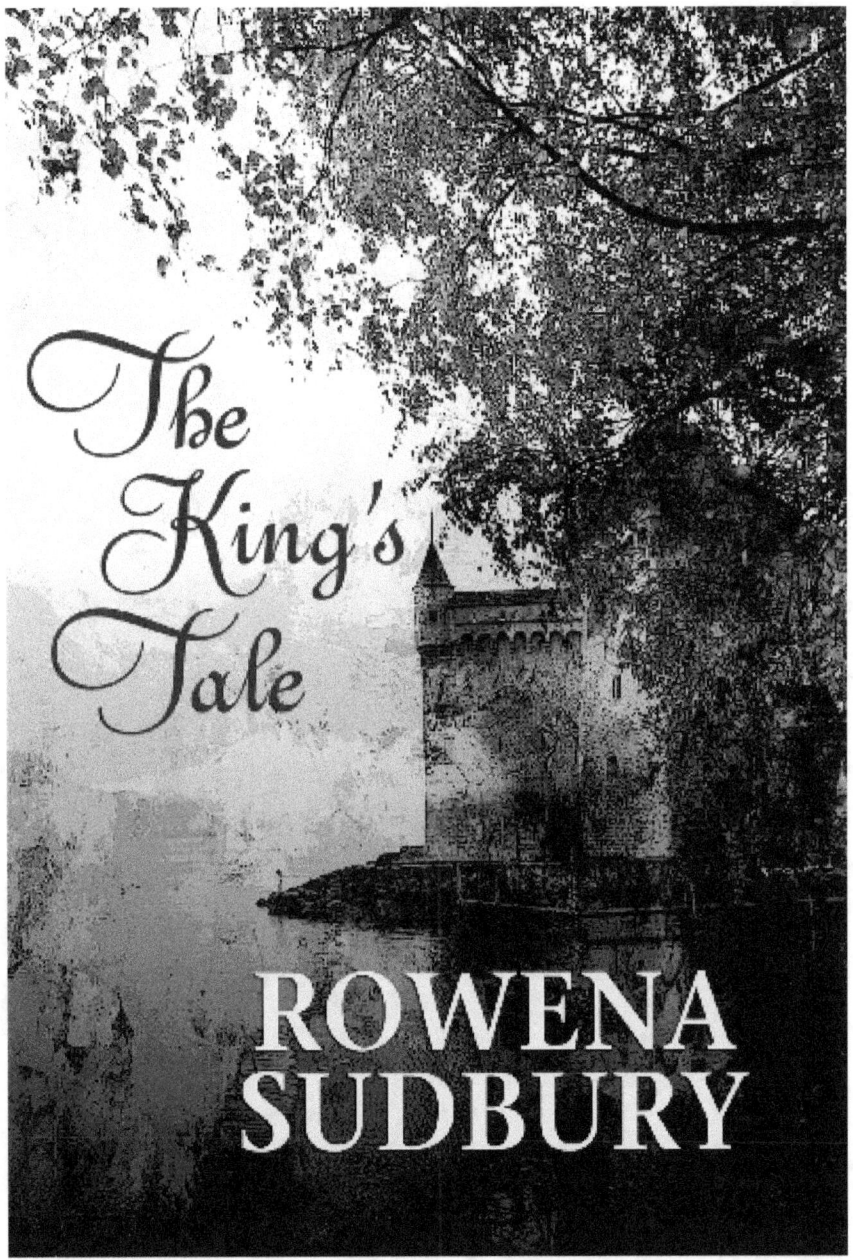

The
King's
Tale

ROWENA
SUDBURY

http://www.dreamspinnerpress.com

Contemporary Romance from DREAMSPINNER PRESS